The Little Blue Boat

AND THE MARSH MAN'S GOLD!

The
Little Blue
Boat

The Little Blue Boat

AND THE MARSH MAN'S GOLD!

PHIL JOHNSON

ILLUSTRATED BY PAUL JACKSON

Matador
9 Priory Business Park,
Wistow Road, Kibworth Beauchamp,
Leicestershire. LE8 0RX
Tel: (+44) 116 279 2299
Fax: (+44) 116 279 2277
Email: books@troubador.co.uk
Web: www.troubador.co.uk/matador

ISBN 978-1783064-861

British Library Cataloguing in Publication Data.
A catalogue record for this book is available from the British Library.

Printed and bound in the UK by TJ International, Padstow, Cornwall
Typeset in 12pt Palatino by Troubador Publishing Ltd, Leicester, UK

Matador is an imprint of Troubador Publishing Ltd

In memory of Milly.

Thanks to Fi.

Thanks also to Nick Crane; Chris Rushby and Caroline Jarrold; Tony Baker at Linden Crescent Marketing; John Marshall at UKTI East; and to my fantastic friends and family for their encouragement.

Special thanks to the Broads Authority and its staff for their continued support, especially the Rangers who showed me the beauty and the secrets of the southern rivers and Broads.

Grateful thanks as well to Paul Jackson for his brilliant illustrations.

The Southern Rivers and Broads – where our story unfolds!

Key:

1 Gt Yarmouth Yacht Station where the crossing begins!
2 The landing stage in the fog!
3 The boat yard where Lucy and Alfie go on alone.
4 The dyke where Pincher Pete steals the cruiser.
5 Where Able Sea Bear Teddy is picked up by the boy.
6 Where Teddy escaped!
7 Where the archaeologist was kidnapped!
8 The wreck of the Viking longboat!
9 Where the driver kept the coypu!
10 Where it all ends!

The water is waiting for you. Explore, enjoy, have fun. Respect the creatures that live there, and remember – **always** wear a lifejacket!

CHAPTER ONE

Out!

It was nightfall in summer. There was tension and the smell of evil in the air. The otter floated in the water as quietly as she could, her warm dark eyes watching, unblinking, her body motionless in the cool water; her nose just twitching above the surface, always ready to dart down and disappear but keen to gather all the information she could. There had been a rumour, a rumour which had rustled through the reeds and rippled over the water. Pincher Pete was out of prison, and he was coming back to the Broads.

Over at Great Yarmouth Yacht Station, *The Little Blue Boat* was tied safely to the quayside. On board Able Sea Bear Teddy lay in the forepeak – that's the sharp front end of the inside of a boat, in boat language. He'd been left there by the children and, although he could move around, he knew he'd have to creep back to where they'd left him when they came back in the morning.

Able Sea Bear Teddy, who came from a long line of Able Sea Bears, was a bit of a special creature. To the children who owned the small yacht, he was simply a mascot; the bear had been owned by Rod, their grandfather, who'd given them the boat when he'd become too old to sail her, but we know different. The Able Sea Bear was special. He could speak all types of animal, bird and fish and even some shell fish – that's modern crustacean of course, not old European crustacean, which has the most complicated series of squeaks which only those with a fine shell can understand, but he could just about get by. He could also speak human, mainly English but a little French and German as well. However, he could never let on to the children or anyone else because, if he did, he feared he would be whisked away to some laboratory as a freak of nature and who knows what might happen to him there.

There was one person he could speak to, and that was the Marsh Man. The Marsh Man knew about Teddy and had helped him escape from Pincher Pete the year before, when *The Little Blue Boat* had first come to the Broads.

Over on the River Yare on the southern rivers, the

otter watched and waited. Soon the dark shape of a scruffy, shaven-headed figure walked out of the bushes and, looking around, spat on the ground before walking into the pub. A few minutes later, a car drew up in the pub's car park. It was black. Three men got out; big men, ugly men, scary men. One, with a hat on, was bigger, uglier and scarier than the others.

The otter shrank back in the water; she tried to make out their faces in the dark evening. Then she lifted her head and gave an eerie squeak, sending her fears across the cool, moist air. It was picked up by the bats who were swooping above the pub, catching their evening meal of insects which they plucked from mid-air. The bats landed on the pub windows and looked through to the scene inside.

Here, lit by low, yellow-tinged light, people in the pub were chatting, laughing and telling jokes, most of them very old jokes. Oh and they were talking about the weather as well; people in pubs often talk about the weather. In the corner of the pub, under a faded painting of the river with an old boat on it, next to the window, Pincher Pete was waiting.

The three men walked up to him carrying drinks they'd just bought at the bar: three big mugs of beer. Without saying anything they sat down around his table, and then the biggest man spoke. The bats couldn't hear what was being said, but they sensed bad things were going to happen.

*

Dawn broke over the golden mile in Great Yarmouth, the warm early summer light started to colour and warm the soft sand, freshly uncovered by the receding tide. On the town's quay, boats laden with timber waited to be unloaded.

Through the Haven Bridge, from where *The Little Blue Boat* had begun her Broads' adventure the year before, the first of the holiday cruisers nosed its way across Breydon Water. At the Great Yarmouth Yacht Station the Broads Navigation Rangers arrived for work, ready to offer to help boats passing up and down the river. *The Little Blue Boat* was about the smallest yacht you could find. Just over four metres long, with two berths – a berth is a bed in boat language – and a small cockpit; that's the bit you sit in at the back. She'd spent the autumn and winter at her new home at Barton Turf on the River Ant, where her new owners had been sprucing her up and learning to sail. The three of them, Lucy now twelve, Sam who's ten and eight-year-old Alfie, had been doing training courses to learn about safety and sailing.

Their dad had also hired an instructor to take them out on *The Little Blue Boat* too, so they all knew how she handled in the water and wind. Every boat is different as the size and position of the sails and the keel, or keels in the case of *The Little Blue Boat*, can differ and so the boat will handle differently. The three children were now ready for a great adventure!

Lucy, Sam and Alfie had spent weeks planning their first voyage. They were going to take *The Little Blue Boat* from her home by Barton Broad and sail her across

Breydon Water to the southern rivers and Broads. They had an aunty who lived in Beccles, a pretty town in Suffolk on the River Waveney, and they were planning to spend a night in her house. Their dad had arranged to hire a motor cruiser to follow their route and keep an eye on them, and he would moor next to them on other nights of the cruise. Planning the journey had taken up much of their time during the Easter holidays. Hours pondering over maps of the Broads and working out where to stay and how long it might take to get there. Lucy was desperate to do the trip without their dad, but that wasn't an option as she was too young and she didn't have enough experience. Learning about boats and the water takes time.

After packing and plotting and finally leaving, they'd completed the first stretch of the journey from Barton Broad, along the River Ant to the River Bure and then under Acle Bridge to the Great Yarmouth Yacht Station. Their dad had insisted they spend the first night on the hire cruiser with him, but once they'd got to the southern rivers across Breydon he was happy to let them take it in turns to sleep on *The Little Blue Boat*. They would have to take it in turns as it could only accommodate two people and a teddy bear as it was so small.

*

Dawn broke over Great Yarmouth and on the south side of Breydon Water the otter was swimming fast, darting in and out of the reeds along the River Yare. She had to get a message through to the Bittern Council. The bats had confirmed her worst fears, Pincher Pete was about and he'd met with some very nasty looking men. She needed to find out what they were planning. She knew that if she could find the Marsh Man he might be able to help.

It's often said in the Broads that you won't find the Marsh Man, but he will find you if he knows you need help or need to talk to him. He's the only human still known to be able to properly understand the animal world and has an incredible ability to share their feelings. Sure enough as the otter swam passed Brundall Marina, she had an instinctive feeling to turn down a small dyke on the southern side of the river. As she entered the narrow, shallow dyke she smelt the comforting scent of the Marsh Man, she knew he was close by.

The otter swam more slowly, flexing her strong tail. Her thick fur was wet and glistening in the early light. Then as she slowed she saw the familiar figure of the Marsh Man, standing in the reeds, his ancient paddle at his side.

"Hello otter, how are you?" said the Marsh Man crouching down to the water's edge.

The otter looked up at him and gave a short, quiet, gentle bark and waved her head to the left.

"Ah I think you're trying to tell me that Pincher Pete is back aren't you? Yes, yes you are." The Marsh Man nodded, understanding. "I wonder what he's planning; I will try to find out, thank you for telling me otter, take care and look after those young otters." With that he turned away, concerned, very concerned.

The otter barked again and spun round, swimming quickly back along the dyke to the open river.

*

"Come on!" said Lucy, trying to get her youngest brother Alfie to finish his breakfast. "The tide's going down, it's almost out and we need to get across Breydon, now!"

There are certain times when it's a good idea to cross Breydon Water and certain times when it's definitely not a good idea to cross Breydon Water, and low tide or low water is the best time. Lucy knew if they missed this chance they'd have to wait twelve hours until the next low tide and she didn't want that.

"OK sister don't get grumpy. You're always grumpy," said Alfie, putting down his empty, just-licked clean spoon.

"And bossy!" added their brother Sam, "You're bossy too!"

"Well someone has to get you boys in order. And, and it's not 'sister' it's SKIPPER."

"Just because you're the oldest," said Sam, "doesn't mean you're the best sailor."

"But I am," snapped Lucy.

"OK OK all of you, Lucy's right we have to cross Breydon while the water's low, let's get going, I'll wash up later," said their dad.

"Who IS the best sailor, Dad?" asked Alfie.

"Well I have to say," he replied slowly and carefully,

"Lucy is pretty good and she does seem to have a natural ability to feel the wind and the water."

"Typical," said Sam.

"But you two are both brilliant as well!" added their dad quickly.

Able Sea Bear Teddy stirred from his dream about the happy days he spent with Rod, the children's granddad, and how they would take *The Little Blue Boat* out on the Essex backwaters for weekend trips. Watching the colourful sails of the old vintage sailing barges ploughing along though the waves, and seeing scores of children on small dinghies racing up and down the nearby estuaries. He heard the children approaching on the quay above them.

The boat, of course, had dropped down as the water level had fallen and it was a steep climb for the three crew – or should that be the skipper and her two crew. All three children and their dad were wearing lifejackets. They had put them on before they left the motor cruiser and climbed up the ladder to the quayside.

The children's dad held the mooring line – that's the rope that ties a boat to the quay, in boat language – and made sure the boat was as close to the quay as it could be so the children could climb down the ladder safely. Once they were all on board he asked the Navigation Rangers to be ready to help cast them off when they were ready; 'casting off' means untying the ropes in boat language. He then got onto his hire cruiser and started the motor.

Above them, a seagull and his gull friend hovered in the thermal currents in the air.

"No chance of a marmite sandwich then?" said the gull to his gull friend.

"Not with that lot on board," she replied.

"Pity," replied her gull friend. "We like sandwiches, especially marmite sandwiches." Below them on the water things were happening. Good things.

The plan was for *The Little Blue Boat*, under the command of Skipper Lucy, to lead the way under the bridges and across Breydon Water, with Dad following in the motor cruiser. Lucy intended to show him they didn't need any help. The mast on *The Little Blue Boat* was lying down across the top of the deck and sticking out over the stern of the boat – that's the back of the boat in boat language. There wasn't much room in the cockpit so Alfie went below to sit with Able Sea Bear Teddy and write the ship's log – that's a sort of diary that boat crews keep to record details of their voyages.

Lucy took the helm – that means holding the tiller, which is the stick used to steer with, or the wheel if a boat has one of those instead. She looked ahead for oncoming boats, behind her for following boats, and checked the state of the tide. She started the small electric outboard motor on the back of the small yacht, then looked around the craft to ensure it was ready for the voyage. Everything was stowed below, or tied safely to the deck so it couldn't fall off once they'd got underway. The mast was lying down so they could go under the low bridges between the yacht station and the open Breydon Water. She also checked that her crew had their lifejackets on. That's essential, anyone can fall from a boat, or the riverbank, quayside or bridges. Even good swimmers need to wear lifejackets or buoyancy aids because the water is cold, and it's wet, which means your clothes will quickly become very heavy and prevent or slow down your swimming. You can of course be knocked out by hitting your head on the boat or anything else as you fall. Always wear a lifejacket.

Lucy shouted to her dad in the cruiser behind.

"Ready to cast off!" she shouted in the most grown up, commanding voice she could find.

"Can you untie us please?" he called to the Rangers on the quay ready to help.

The Rangers untied both boats and threw the ropes back to them. "Watch your speed and have a good day," they said as they waved goodbye.

With that the two boats were freed from the captivity of the quay ready for an adventure; and what an adventure it was going to be. They had no idea as they slowly made their way down the River Bure to Breydon Water just what lay ahead in the days to come.

CHAPTER TWO

Fog!

'Limit of Navigation' read the large sign before the Haven Bridge at Great Yarmouth.

"That means us!" noted Alfie peering out from the small front hatch of *The Little Blue Boat.* Lucy turned the tiller to point the boat in the opposite direction and towards the bascule bridge, which spans the eastern entrance to Breydon Water.

"Yes," added his brother Sam, sitting in the cockpit next to Lucy, "it's to stop hire craft and other boats from going out to sea."

"Why?" asked Alfie.

"Because," said Lucy, "because – and you should know this! – unless you are equipped for sea and capable of sailing at sea you shouldn't go. The tides can be fierce, the waves dangerous and the sandbanks and underwater obstacles a complete nightmare. Besides most hire craft and river boats have shallow keels, and that means there's not enough sticking down under the water to stop them from being tipped over in waves and wind."

"This boat's been to sea," said Alfie,

"Yes," replied Sam, "but only on a carefully planned

voyage by Granddad, and it's actually a bit small to have done that."

"Can we go to sea one day?" asked Alfie.

"Perhaps," smiled Lucy. "I really hope Dad will let us one day."

"Do you think I should put Teddy on deck?" asked Alfie.

Oh yes, yes please! said Teddy to himself, stuck inside the cabin staring at the white walls which stared back at him. *A bear could go stir crazy down here, especially an Able Sea Bear,* he said to himself.

Alfie pulled the small bear up through the hatch and, after checking his lifejacket was firmly on, Alfie put Teddy on the very front of the boat, but tied him to the forward cleat with a piece of cord specially there for that purpose.

"There you go Teddy, now you can see where we're going," smiled Alfie.

If I could thank you I would, said Teddy to himself, *but then you'd know I could talk and that would never do.*

The small yacht with the three children and Able Sea Bear Teddy passed under the bridge with traffic thundering across it above them, and then the wide expanse of Breydon Water lay before them.

"Lucy," called the children's dad from the motor cruiser, which had been following very close behind. "Lucy can you slow down, I'll overtake and tie to the metal posts then you can come alongside me and we'll raise the mast."

The bridge operator watched as the motor cruiser

carefully stopped beside a large metal post called a 'dolphin', which had been specially put there so boats could stop to raise and lower their masts. He threw a rope around it and tied it so the motor cruiser couldn't move, and then, as Lucy brought *The Little Blue Boat* alongside the motor cruiser, he grabbed the wooden grab rails on the small yacht's coach roof and, as he held the boats together, Sam quickly tied a rope to the

cruiser, the fenders lined up along its side rubbed gently against the small yacht's hull.

"Right, let's raise the mast," said Dad, and he watched, smiling as his three children performed the simple but practised manoeuvre to perfection.

"I'll get the sails," shouted Alfie smiling, and dropped back through the hatch into the cabin.

Teddy stared ahead, he saw something flash before him, it was a bird, flying fast and furiously, and a flash of bright electric blue passed by.

"Look!" shouted Lucy, "It's a kingfisher! They're usually seen by the banks."

The children and their dad stopped and watched as the shy bird darted around the boat. What they didn't hear or see was its message to Able Sea Bear Teddy. In short sharp bursts it swopped down and said, "Teddy. I've an urgent message from the otter…" flying up and then returning quickly the bird rapidly passed on the next bit of the message. "Pincher Pete…" up again went the bird flashing its colours in the milky sunlight. "He's back and up to no good. Beware little bear, beware!" With that the kingfisher took to the sky then darted down and swooped across the water's surface to the bushes beyond the reeds. Teddy looked worried.

The children finished rigging the boat and then untied themselves from the motor cruiser. Moving off under the power of the electric motor, Lucy turned the boat so it was pointing in to the wind, which was very gentle, and Sam pulled up the main sail. Alfie closed the front hatch and went below, emerging to sit on the step between the cockpit and the cabin. Sam pulled up the jib sail – or front sail – and Lucy switched off the electric motor. She then turned the boat gently so the wind filled the sails.

"Wow we're off!" shouted Sam,

"Yes under sail too," added Alfie.

"Pull that jib rope tight please crew!" said Lucy in a firm but friendly way. The jib rope, or jib sheet to give it its proper name, is the bit of rope that's attached to the bottom of the front sail. Jib sails have two ropes from the bottom so you can sit in the cockpit and pull the sail to the left or right, depending on which way the wind is coming from. A big jib, or front sail, is called a 'genoa'. There are lots of funny names in boat language.

The little yacht, followed by the motor cruiser, began the voyage across Breydon Water. The tide was low and the water slack, soon it would begin to come in from the sea and help push the boats up the river. Something else was coming in too, a sea mist, so thick it was fog. Soon the two boats would be lost in the large stretch of open water bounded on all sides by low lying marsh and reeds. Before the reeds and marsh though was mud: thick, dangerous mud.

*

On the River Yare down a small dyke, Pincher Pete was walking along a row of carefully moored boats, empty and resting, waiting for their owners to take them out for a sail or motor up the river. Sadly Pincher Pete was going to take one of these boats out, without permission, and the boat wouldn't enjoy the trip. No, not at all.

Walking down the dyke he looked for the easiest boat to steal. Now crime is very rare on the Broads. River people keep a look out for each other's boats and the Rangers and the Broads Beat Police Officers are always on the lookout for anything suspicious, but on this day, Pincher Pete was about to go back to his bad old ways. Pincher Pete had been arrested for stealing *The Little Blue Boat* almost a year ago.

"You are an habitual offender," the Magistrate had told him when he was in court, and Pincher Pete was sentenced to six months in prison. He'd pleaded guilty to six other offences so prison was where he went. Now he was out, but he hadn't learned his lesson.

Pincher Pete found an easy target; a little motor cruiser with no locks on the door. Looking around quickly to ensure there was no one about, he jumped in and opened the door to the cabin. There, hanging up, were the keys.

"Oh this is so easy!" grinned Pincher Pete, wiping his running nose on his old fleece, the sleeve of which was hard and crusty from the rest of the countless times he'd done the very same thing. He switched on the fuel and turned the key. The old but well maintained diesel engine with its two cylinders started up with a cough and a splutter. He listened for the sound of water pumping out at the back of the boat. This was the water being pumped round the engine to keep it cool and stop it from overheating. '*Splurt splurt splurt*' it went as the water went back into the river from where it had been pumped.

Pincher Pete waved to the car parked nearby and two of the three men he'd met in the pub the night before walked quickly down to the boat and jumped in. The car started up and drove off.

"Is this it?" asked the first man, looking around, his ugly face screwed up.

"Best for the moment," replied Pincher Pete. "We'll nick one of those big boys later, you know one of those 'gin palaces'. I nicked one once, got it up the river at twenty miles an hour, crashed it and ran off. We'll do that later."

"After," said the other bigger, ugly man, his face thin with a large scar across his fat neck, "after we've got the goods. Just don't, and I mean DON'T, 'urt my 'at. Understand?"

"I won't hurt your hat boss," said Pincher Peter gulping. He was now very scared.

Pincher Pete untied the ropes and the two men with him pushed the wooden posts on the quay to get the boat moving. The three villains chugged up the dyke towards the River Yare. One of them pulled the ring on a can of larger and started gulping it down. The other lit a cigarette, offering one to Pincher Pete, who grinned and deliberately turned the wheel hard to the left to make the little motor boat hit another moored boat.

"Like dodgems this is!" he laughed.

A moorhen had been watching and quickly swam

off to warn others what was going on. The otter, who had been dozing and dreaming of fish and her planned summer holiday visit to her cousins on the northern rivers, was suddenly aware of the short, high-pitched shriek of the moorhen.

Oh no he's on the water. I'd better find him and follow him, she said to herself and swam out of the reeds.

The stolen boat chugged on. Pincher Pete was deliberately keeping the speed down so as not to attract attention. The boat passed the otter as she came out of the reeds. She knew it was the thief as his shape and looks were well known across the Broads. The otter followed, swimming as fast as she could behind them.

*

"Where did THIS come from?" asked Sam as the fog swarmed around *The Little Blue Boat* as it crossed Breydon Water.

"I'm not sure, it's pretty rare but it can happen even in the summer," shouted his dad in the cruiser behind. "It wasn't forecast or we'd never have started the crossing," he continued.

"Better start the motor and then take the sails down," said Lucy, turning the boat into the wind, which had now almost died away. "Let's drop the sails then," she said to her brothers, who quickly followed her command and took the sails down and tied them up.

Teddy sat watching the view disappear under a

thick, dense cloud of tiny droplets of water vapour, or fog as we call it.

The boats continued very slowly. Breydon Water is very shallow at the edges. There are posts to show you where the safe areas are, but in fog these are hard to see. If you go outside of these posts there's a good chance you could become stuck on the mud. Thick, gooey mud, which will hold on to you until the tide lifts you off it. Sometimes though, the tide doesn't. In fog your sense of direction can get confused. The children's dad called out from the cruiser for the children to stay close and announced he would take them in tow so they could stay together. *The Little Blue Boat* though had already gone off course. Lucy had over steered, pushing the tiller too far to the left – or to port in boat language – and had drifted away from her dad and the cruiser. Fog can do funny things to sound as well and their dad thought they were on the other side and turned the other way. The two boats spread apart.

"Over here!" called Sam.

"We're here!" shouted Alfie getting worried.

Calm down, calm down said Able Sea Bear Teddy to himself. *The worst thing you can do is panic. Keep a clear head, don't all shout at once and listen for a reply.* He shook his head a little, wishing he could tell the children what to do.

"Where are you?" called their dad, now getting worried and wishing he'd tied them to the cruiser earlier.

The fog got thicker and the tide began to rush in

through the river mouth at Great Yarmouth. The incoming water increased in speed and volume, pushing the boats further along and towards danger. The usually pretty open water had suddenly become full of unseen hazards. The muddy shallows, posts, bits of old landing stages and underwater obstacles lay ahead. Each and any of them could do serious damage to *The Little Blue Boat* and to the cruiser too. Water and nature has to be respected and what can one minute be safe and relaxing can the next be a potential problem. The children were now in danger, and so was their dad.

CHAPTER THREE

Ouch!

The kingfisher swooped down through the fog and found *The Little Blue Boat*. The children, who were all in the cockpit and on the step, didn't notice. The bird landed next to Teddy.

"You're in trouble," said the bird.

"Oh I know, why do we let humans out in boats hey? If only Able Sea Bears were the *only* creatures allowed to be in charge of vessels, life would be so much easier," said the bear shaking his head.

"That may be the case," replied the kingfisher, "but they are in charge. Now then, I have put out an all beaks tweet so everyone knows that you're in trouble. Try to get the children to go to the old landing stage on the right over there; it's not far, I know it well."

"That's easier said than done," said the Able Sea Bear. "Umm… it is dangerous but I have a plan. Can you undo this cord holding me in place please?"

"You're not going to take over and shock them are you?"

"No, no," said Teddy, "I need to be free. Go, and watch what happens."

With that the bird took the cord in its beak and

undid the knot. The bird flew off. "Good luck bear," it said as it darted off to the clear skies above the fog.

Teddy said to himself, *This is dangerous but it's my duty to help the children.* With that, the brave but foolish bear threw himself off the front of the slow moving boat into the water below. As he did he kicked the hull making a loud thump.

"NO!" shouted Alfie, "Teddy's fallen in!"

"Teddy overboard!" shouted Sam loudly.

Lucy stopped the boat's motor and began to circle. "Sam you keep visual sight on Teddy. Do not lose sight of him! Alfie, grab the fishing net NOW!"

The girl skipper turned the boat gently to come alongside the floating bear, safe in his lifejacket but being carried away by the incoming tide. Teddy swam, but without them knowing, he kicked his legs and swam towards the landing stage, which he'd been told was there by the kingfisher.

"If we go too far this way," said Lucy, "we'll hit the mud and be stuck!"

"We might be wrecked!" said Alfie.

"But we have to try and get Teddy back," said Sam desperately.

As *The Little Blue Boat* moved closer and closer to the landing stage, Teddy was carried away further by the tide. He was soon out of sight.

"NO!" shouted Sam, "I've lost sight of him!"

"But wait," said Lucy, "look there's a landing stage."

Out of the fog formed the shape of the old wooden landing stage, high out of the water. On it stood a man

Ouch!

holding a paddle. Above the man a kingfisher flew in circles then darted off in the direction of Teddy.

"Ahoy," shouted the man. "If you head for me I can grab your rope and you will be safe."

"It's a stranger," said Alfie, worried.

"But there are three of us, and we're in a boat, and we're in danger in the fog," said Lucy.

"He seems OK," said Sam, standing up to his full height ready for a fight if he had to.

Lucy brought *The Little Blue Boat* alongside the wooden landing stage; she had to use the electric motor flat out to hold the boat against the tide until the man grabbed the rear and then the front ropes, and tied the boat up safely.

"Hello, I'm Lucy and these are my brothers, Sam and Alfie. Who are you?"

"They call me the Marsh Man," smiled the man, holding his hand up as if to wave and show he meant no harm.

Across Breydon Water the sound of powerful diesel engines could be heard, a boat was ploughing through the fog. The children's dad had used his mobile to call the Broads Authority and report their situation. Within minutes the Rangers' boat, *Spirit of Breydon*, had been alerted and had changed course from patrolling the River Waveney and had gone to help.

The cruiser had been quickly found. The Rangers on *Spirit of Breydon* started searching for *The Little Blue Boat* and, within minutes, the children, now safely on the landing stage, heard the sound of a friendly voice booming out from a loudspeaker. Lights cut through the fog and the Broads Authority patrol boat slowly came into view out of the dense mist. Alfie turned to the Marsh Man, but he'd gone. He was simply nowhere to be seen.

"Over here!" shouted Lucy

"WE'RE HERE!" echoed Alfie.

Sam, who had walked to the edge of the landing stage, ran back quickly, too quickly. He slipped on the wet wood and fell. He fell badly, very badly. He fell through a piece of rotten planking and twisted his ankle, smashing it and banging it against metal and wood.

"OUCH! Ahhh! I've really hurt myself, really, really." Poor old Sam was holding back the tears as his ankle began to swell and hurt like heck.

Soon *The Little Blue Boat* and the cruiser were at the boat yard base of *Spirit of Breydon*, a little way up the River Waveney at the southern end of Breydon Water. They were now tide up safely on the quayside. The fog had lifted. Sam was in real pain. A paramedic was on the way. The Rangers thought he may have broken his ankle, so it was off to hospital for an x-ray.

Oh what a mess, thought Teddy, floating on the tide in his lifejacket; his fur cold and wet. "At least the children are safe," he said out loud.

"That's true," said the Marsh Man, "and you're safe too my little friend."

Teddy looked round and there was the Marsh Man rowing a small boat, the kingfisher flying above them.

Soon Teddy was drying out in the Marsh Man's boat, as he was rowed to the shore.

"Thank you!" said Teddy, grateful to be rescued by his friend.

"It's what I do," smiled the Marsh Man.

The fog began to lift as they entered the River Yare and headed for a small opening in the reeds just beyond the Berney Arms pub. The Marsh Man rowed the small, old boat into the reeds away from prying eyes, and then put the oars down and looked at Able Sea Bear Teddy.

"We have a problem," he said.

"I know," said Teddy, "Pincher Pete is back."

"And he has a gang with him. A gang that are after something, and we need to find out what that is. I hope it's not the ancient gold," said the Marsh Man slowly.

"Ancient gold?" enquired Teddy puzzled.

"There's a legend that a Viking longboat sank hundreds of years ago on a river near here and it has gold on board."

"WOW!" said Teddy. "Do you know where it is?"

"I might," replied the Marsh Man. "I might have known for... a very long time," he added.

"How could they know?" asked Teddy.

"They might not, it might be something different, and that's what you have got to find out Teddy."

The kingfisher took off, leaving the two in the boat making plans and embarking on a mission to find Pincher Pete and his ruthless, evil pals.

*

A few miles further up the River Yare the very same Pincher Pete and his pals were on board the small stolen cruiser. Another boat passed, then, turned to follow them.

"What do they want?" asked the man with the hat.

"I'll ask," sneered Pincher Pete.

The other motor cruiser came along next to them; an old man leaned out of the cockpit and waved.

"Hello, sorry to bother you, but that's Linda and Bill's boat, are they here? They don't usually come on their boat in July, they're usually in Spain," he said.

"Er, that's right," said Pincher Pete, "they said we could borrow it."

"Oh, OK then, have fun," replied the man and turned his boat around to continue back to the dyke where it lived. He turned to his wife who was inside the cabin making tea.

"I think we ought to check with Linda and Bill as it's unusual for them to lend the boat and those three didn't look like the sort of people who'd be friends of theirs."

Pincher Pete motored on passed Reedham then went under the swing bridge and soon turned the small stolen cruiser down the Haddiscoe New Cut, a canal which linked the River Yare with the River Waveney.

"What a boring, dull bit of river," said the smaller of the ugly men sitting next to Pincher Pete.

"If I get my hat damaged you will be to blame," said the bigger of the two, with the scar on his chin. "I need my hat to cover my face," he added.

"It's ugly," sneered Pincher Pete,

"You saying my face is ugly?" said the bigger of the men, the boss.

"No, oh no, not your face, the river is ugly," said Pincher Pete. "Your face is very pretty."

"Pretty?!" said the boss.

"Not pretty, er it's just right. This bit of river is a short cut, but it's as ugly as you... er I mean as ugly as you can get," he gulped.

*

"So is it broken then?" asked the children's dad, standing by his son Sam in the Accident and Emergency department of the hospital.

"Luckily for you young lad it's not broken but it's a very bad sprain," nodded the doctor looking at the x-ray on the screen. "You gave it quite a whack young man. You're going to have it bandaged and need to keep a cold compress on it to reduce the swelling. You need to go home, go to bed and rest for a few days."

"What?!" gasped Sam, feeling very angry with himself.

"Yes, it has to mend properly. It will take a while," said the doctor, washing his hands.

"He's on a sailing trip for ten days at the moment," said Sam's dad.

"Sorry, he can't go on a boat like this, he won't have the movement and he can't put pressure on the foot or ankle, he'll need crutches to get about and he mustn't get it wet either. I'm sorry but you'll have to sit this one out."

"Sorry Dad," said Sam, feeling very stupid having fallen and hurt his ankle.

"Well Sam it's back to Auntie's house for you. I'm sorry but you're going to miss the trip," replied his dad. "At least it's not broken," he added.

Back at the boat yard, close to where the River Waveney joins Breydon Water, *The Little Blue Boat* was being given a tidy up by Lucy and Alfie. They looked up when they heard a car stopping by the boat sheds. It was their auntie's car; she had met them at the hospital and was dropping their dad off before driving Sam back to her house in Beccles. He waved to Lucy and Alfie who waved back and could see two crutches sticking up on the back seat.

The children and their dad sat on the motor cruiser eating cake. It was agreed after a lot of arguing, pleading and even some proper emergency crying by Lucy, that Dad would go to their auntie's house in Beccles on the cruiser. Lucy and Alfie would be allowed to carry on and take *The Little Blue Boat* to Beccles to their auntie's house, and meet up with them but only if they phoned four times a day and moored up in places where their dad could come and find them at night, and stay with them or at least stop close by.

It was agreed that tonight they would stay at the river centre, a marina with a campsite on the River Waveney where Dad could pitch a tent. An hour later Lucy and Alfie were alone in *The Little Blue Boat*; their dad had motored off to Beccles in the cruiser. He would moor it on the quay there and then drive back to meet them for the night.

"I miss Teddy," said Alfie.

"I know, it's really sad," replied Lucy, feeling a great loss inside.

"Do you think we'll ever see him again?" asked Alfie, the tears forming in his eyes.

"Oh I hope so, he did have a lifejacket on and someone may hand him in to the Rangers. Dad did ask them to keep a look out for him and they promised to tell their friends who patrol the River Yare so let's hope so."

"I bet he's out there somewhere, lost in the reeds, washed up and wet, and with no one to love him," said Alfie, crying softly.

"Come on crew let's try to sail this bit shall we?" said Lucy, trying to be grown up and change the subject.

"I miss Mum you know," said Alfie, pulling up the main sail as Lucy turned the boat into the wind.

"We all do Alfie, we all do."

"Dad's great at helping with school stuff and things and he's great to talk to as well," replied Alfie, tying off the main halyard – that's the rope which pulls up the main sail in boat language.

"I know he is," said Lucy, "but girls need to talk to their mums sometimes. They just do. Come let's get that jib up, and pull it out to the port side, there's a bit of wind!"

"OK," said Alfie and after setting the sail he turned

to look back, hoping beyond hope to catch sight of the little yacht's Able Sea Bear, now officially lost at sea. They had started out with a crew of three and a ship's bear, now there were just two of them with no bear. Alfie suddenly went cold. *Could it get worse?* he asked himself.

Across the reeds on the Haddiscoe New Cut were Pincher Pete and the two ugly criminals on the stolen motor cruiser; three bad men with evil plans. Yes, things could get worse, much worse.

CHAPTER FOUR

Grabbed!

A mile away on the River Yare, Teddy was sitting in a hollowed-out log; a sort of mini canoe with a small paddle-shaped stick. The Marsh Man had made it for him. The Marsh Man had pushed him out into the river and he was going to try and track down Pincher Pete, helped by any sightings from the birds, animals and fish that lived in the area.

The latest word from the riverbank was that the stolen boat was heading down the Haddiscoe New Cut so Teddy should follow their route in the hope of tracking them down. The problem was he couldn't go very fast. Help, though, was at hand. A grass snake slithered across the water in front of him. Teddy gasped.

"Wow, sorry, you scared me!" said Teddy looking at the greenish brown snake with its yellowish ring around its neck.

"I've been watching, been listening, been waiting," hissed the snake.

"What, under the water?" asked the bear.

"Yes we can stay under the water for an hour, you know, us grass snakes. I've been asked to give you a tow."

"And so have I," said another snake behind him, "I've also been asked to give you a push!"

"Wow," said Teddy as his little log was suddenly being propelled through the water at such a fast rate that it left quite a wake behind it.

Teddy was travelling up the River Yare, which is one of the main rivers of the Broads system. The river is deep and was used in the past for boats taking things like wood, grain, coal and so on between Norwich and Great Yarmouth. The river actually starts near a place called Dereham – or East Dereham to give it its proper name – which is further inland from Norwich. It's around thirty miles between Great Yarmouth and Norwich, and the river, which is affected by the tides, is quite wide in places.

There are some beautiful mills and villages on its banks. Teddy was enjoying the view. He'd just gone passed Polkeys Mill, which is an old drainage mill; a wind pump which was built to pump water from the land into the river to stop the land from flooding and allow farmers to use it for crops and animals. Today it's been restored

and is open for people to have a look around and see how we used to do things many years ago.

Teddy was enjoying the view and as he got closer the mill seemed to rise higher and higher. As he got closer, towering above him was what looked like a giant propeller. These were the old wooden sails, which turn in the wind to allow the water to be pumped into the river from the land. They looked very big and white against the wide open Norfolk sky. But Teddy's thoughts and his view were suddenly snatched away from him, as a hand grabbed his neck!

"Got it Dad!" shouted a small boy, leaning over the back of a holiday cruiser.

"Well done Jack," said a man at the wheel.

"Can we keep it?!" asked the boy.

Teddy had been spotted sitting on his log by a family on holiday. The snakes darted under the water, they couldn't help Teddy, all they could do was get a message back to the Marsh Man that Teddy had been taken.

The brightly coloured cruiser headed up the river towards the village of Reedham. Teddy was stunned but kept dead still and his mouth firmly shut.

Oh no what now?! he thought to himself. *I'll never find Pincher Pete now, or be reunited with the children.* The Able Sea Bear was worried, very worried indeed.

The cruiser passed under Reedham Swing Bridge. It's a lovely old railway bridge which swings open to allow tall boats and yachts with fixed masts to pass through on their way along the river.

"Shall we stop for ice cream?" asked the man at the wheel.

"Oh yes please!" said the small boy, clutching the worried Able Sea Bear.

With that his dad steered the cruiser to the quayside and, helped by a Broads Authority Ranger, it was soon safely tied up. The tide here can make stopping and mooring up quite difficult at times, so the Rangers are always happy to help when they can.

Licking an ice cream from the local shop and sitting on the side of the boat, the small boy asked again, "Can I keep him Dad please, please?"

"Well not really he's obviously someone else's teddy bear; look, he's even got his own life jacket."

"Not fair, finders keepers," said the boy, stuffing the ice cream into his mouth.

"You've got your own teddy bear," said his mum, walking back to the boat from the shop with bread and milk and a rather nice looking chocolate cake for later.

"Yes but I want THIS one!" said the boy stamping his feet.

"Come on," said the boy's dad, starting the cruiser's motor again. "We'll press on; we said we'd have a look at Loddon." With that the boy's mum untied the mooring ropes and the cruiser motored off along the river under the watchful eye of the Ranger who was standing on the quay waving them off.

Just passed Reedham on the way towards Norwich is the River Chet. Near its mouth, where it joins the River Yare, is a large old cross, called the Hardley Cross.

"What's that?!" asked the boy as the Hardley Cross came into view.

"Let's have a look in the guidebook, hold on, would you read it out to us darling?" the boy's dad asked, handing the guidebook to his wife sitting by the boy.

"Yes of course, where are we, oh yes. Er it was built in 1676 to mark the ancient boundary between the boroughs of Norwich and Great Yarmouth. Oh that's interesting," she added and carried on reading the guidebook out loud. "The river also has a wonderful footpath running alongside it called the Wherryman's Way which goes for some thirty-five miles between Norwich and Great Yarmouth and gives people the chance to follow the route which the old trading wherries took. The wherries were the local type of sailing barge, which transported things along the rivers in these parts. Their two-man crews would sail these heavy old boats back and forth, and if there was no wind they would use a huge stick called a 'quant pole' and stick it into water and down to the river bottom to push the craft along. The railways came and the wherries were put out of business, too slow to compete with the fast steam trains which took their business and their jobs. Luckily some of these majestic old ladies of the Broads have been restored and are still on the water today, run by enthusiasts who maintain and love them."

"Well," said the man, "we'll have to look out for them!"

"And for more floating teddies!" said the boy giggling. *Oh dear now what will happen to me?* thought Able Sea

Bear Teddy to himself, held firmly in the grip of the boy's hand.

As the holiday cruiser entered the meandering River Chet to travel the three and a half miles to Loddon, the high-pitched squeak of a peewit could be heard.

Soon they passed the famous Hardley Flood, which is next to the river. It used to be farmland but was flooded some years ago. It's shallow and attracts many wading birds. Before long the cruiser, with the small boy clutching the Able Sea Bear, who they had plucked from the water, came to a row of moored boats at Pyes Mill moorings. The family manoeuvred their floating holiday home alongside, in a space between two other craft. They wanted to stay here for the night. The open grassy bank was a great place to stop. It was named after a mill which used to be here. It's just a short walk to Loddon where there are shops and cafés.

Teddy was getting very worried. He needed to get back to his very important mission, to track down Pincher Pete and find out what he was up to. Sadly he'd been plucked from his log canoe and was being held in forced captivity by this, well-meaning but irritating small boy. He had to think of a plan. Then it came to him, but before he could do anything, the boy's mum announced they were all going off for tea and cakes in Loddon. Teddy felt his arm being grabbed and was soon pulled up and thrust under the small boy's arm as the child stepped off the cruiser and followed his mum and dad along the path to the small town a quarter of a mile away.

The three holidaymakers walked in to Loddon. There at the end of the river, where boats were lined up at the public moorings, they saw a pretty little tea shop, and in they went taking Able Sea Bear Teddy with them. Eating lovely lumps of chocolate cake and drinking mugs of tea, the conversation had once again turned to the future of Teddy.

"But I found him!" protested the boy when his dad said he ought to hand in him 'somewhere' but not quite knowing where you handed in lost teddies. The boy was distraught at the prospect of giving up his new-found treasure and cried loudly, saying repeatedly "Not fair, not fair."

His mother sighed and said, "OK Jack, if no one says it's theirs by the time we go home, then you can keep him."

"Can we go home tonight then?" asked the boy.

"No!" said his dad laughing, and added, "We're going home the day after tomorrow anyway."

The boy put Teddy under his sweatshirt, determined to make sure no one else would see him and would be able to ask for him back.

Teddy was upset, mainly because he was scared of ending up in the boy's bedroom and never seeing the children or *The Little Blue Boat* again. He was also upset because the boy's sweatshirt was really, really smelly, and bears have a good sense of smell, even teddy bears.

An hour later they were back on the holiday cruiser, the evening was coming and the boy was sitting at the back of the boat. The Able Sea Bear was stuffed on a shelf in a back cabin where the boy had been sleeping. Checking no one was about and the door was closed, he climbed up to the window and, using all his strength, pushed the glass sideways with his paws, opening it just enough to stick his head out.

He spotted something in the water. It was like a watery guinea pig with a round head and fat little body swimming gently near the boat. It was a water vole.

"Hey, excuse me," said Teddy in a whisper.

"Me? You want me?" asked the vole.

"Hello, yes, sorry but please help. I need you to organise a rescue mission, I'm Able Sea Bear Teddy."

"I know, the snakes have been looking for you, so have many others. How can I help?"

"Can you fetch a swan or two; I saw some down the river a way back. Can you tell them to come here and…" Teddy whispered his plan to the vole, which blinked, smiled and ducked under the water, swimming off in search of swans.

Teddy waited, and watched and waited. Soon two large white swans swam gracefully up the river to the side of the holiday cruiser. The boy's mum gave her son a biscuit to break up and give to the beautiful birds who were doing their most appealing '*look at me I'm hungry*' act, which many of them practise during the winter months.

The boy broke up a piece of biscuit and leaned over the boat to offer it to the swans but decided it was too good and would eat it himself. He'd already had cake and a few biscuits but he didn't want the swans to have one. The swans, though, knew the boy's mum had asked him to give it to them, so as it was just disappearing into his mouth the first swan leapt up, stuck his long neck over the side of the boat and grabbed the biscuit.

"Wow! It bit me!" screamed the boy.

"I'm sure it didn't," replied his mum, smiling.

"It did!" and with that the boy saw Teddy sitting beside him. "That's funny I left you on my bed," said the boy quietly. He was confused and surprised, but not half as surprised as when the second swan made a sudden movement and hissed loudly right next to the boy's ears. The boy jumped up squealing. As he did the first swan reached in to the boat and grabbed the Able Sea Bear by his lifejacket and swiftly, with his powerful neck, placed Teddy on his friend's back. Then, sitting holding on to the bottom of the swan's neck, Teddy made his escape.

Before the boy or his parents could do anything, the two swans went for an emergency take off and, running along the water's surface at great speed, they gracefully and gently rose into the air, their wide majestic wings flapping in unison. Teddy clung onto the swan's neck not daring to look down. On the water's surface, a smiling vole had watched the whole thing. "Perfect," it said to itself.

The boy pointed and cried, his dad told him it wasn't his teddy in the first place, but it was rather amazing that it had been stolen by a pair of swans.

CHAPTER FIVE

Ruthless!

Lucy and Alfie sailed *The Little Blue Boat* from the boat yard near Burgh Castle, close to the remains of the Roman fort, along the River Waveney to the river centre at Burgh St Peter. On the way they passed mills, marshes and bridges.

It was a perfect July day; the wind was light, but strong enough to fill the blue sails of the small yacht. Lucy let her youngest brother Alfie take the tiller and steer the boat for long stretches along the winding, welcoming river. Holiday cruisers and other yachts passed them by, but Lucy and Alfie were in no hurry. They just had to reach the river centre at Burgh St Peter before nightfall where their dad would be waiting. He was pitching a tent there in the campsite by the marina, and so would be able to check they were OK and take them to eat in a café that evening.

*

Sam was feeling very sorry for himself. Sitting in the narrow garden of his aunt's house, which ran down to the River Waveney in the lovely town of Beccles, he kept re-running the accident in his mind. Why had he run over the wet, slippery wooden landing stage? If he'd taken his time he wouldn't have slipped. That was so painful. Here he was with a big swollen ankle, and worst of all, he was away from his brother and sister and *The Little Blue Boat* and their big adventure. He would see them soon though, his auntie's garden ran down to the river and had a small bit of quay heading on which *The Little Blue Boat* could stop and moor up.

*

Dusk was approaching as Lucy took the tiller from Alfie and, having taken down the sails and started the small electric outboard motor, its battery charged from the

solar panel on the coach roof of the boat, steered the small yacht onto a visitors' pontoon at the marina. Standing waiting to catch the boat and tie her up was their dad.

"All OK?" he shouted, holding out his hands for Alfie to throw him a rope.

"Yes Dad it's been great!" said Alfie "Catch!" and threw him the boat's front, or bow line; then the one from the back.

"How's Sam?" asked Lucy as her dad tied the ropes to the pontoon.

"He's pretty unhappy and in a bit of pain," said their dad, shaking his head gently.

"That's so sad," said Alfie, who was missing his elder brother.

*

Across the marshes, Able Sea Bear Teddy was still firmly gripping the neck of the swan, its powerful wings gently flapping in the sunset red sky. Teddy had just been rescued by the swans from the holiday cruiser, where the small boy had plucked him from his little canoe on the river. It had been a very long day. The bear yawned and started to doze. Now when you're being given a lift by a swan the thing you must always do is hang on. Swans aren't used to running passenger services and these two suddenly veered off to the right. Teddy veered off to the left, and lost his grip. Luckily, the swans weren't flying very high but it seemed a long way to Teddy as he felt the firm feathers of the swan slip through his paws. Now bears don't fly too well. In fact they can't fly at all. Soon the ground got closer and closer. Below Teddy were reeds and a small cruiser moored by a tiny stretch of grassy riverbank.

"Ahh!" mumbled the Able Sea Bear. "I wish I had a parachute!" But he didn't.

Down and down he fell.

"Oh," said a coot, swimming with its mate along the river, "no one forecast raining bears today?"

"Must be a freak bear storm," said its mate as they swam for cover.

There was a bump as the small bear hit the ground. Luckily for the Able Sea Bear he fell into a big patch of reeds; he crashed through them and landed on a damp, soft mud floor below.

Oh where am I? That was scary, thought the bear. He felt a bit sore but luckily nothing was broken. Teddy scratched his head and looked through the reeds to see a small motor cruiser. There on the cruiser eating cold meat pies were Pincher Pete, the big ugly man with the hat and the smaller ugly man. Teddy recognised Pincher Pete's voice and carefully picked his way through the reeds to get closer and have a listen to what they were saying.

The spot where Teddy had landed, and the cruiser with Pincher Pete and the gang on board, was only a very short distance from the river centre where Lucy, Alfie and *The Little Blue Boat* were staying.

On the riverbank in the stolen cruiser, Pincher Pete

was being told of his mission by the big bad man with the hat, which he never took off.

"Pete, pass that whiskey, the bottle we stole from that little old lady's car outside the supermarket."

"That was easy," said his fellow gang member, "she hadn't even locked her car. Pity there was nothing more interesting in her shopping than these meat pies, some bread and milk."

"Yes," said Pincher Pete, "but there's tea and coffee in the boat."

"Good job," said the boss, touching his hat. "Good job people are decent enough to leave us thieves things to use in their boats isn't it!" They all laughed as the smaller of the gang stubbed his cigarette out on the lovely polished wooden surface of the little motor cruiser.

Teddy had crawled forward and was watching through the cruiser's window, desperately hoping he wouldn't be seen. He saw and heard everything and felt sick. How could people be so horrible and so nasty? He listened on.

"So this is the plan Pincher Pete, " said the boss, "when I was in prison for the last bank job, I was in a jail not far from here. I met one of these prison visitors he was an arechaeo... archy... archi... archaeologist thingy person."

"Oh someone who digs up old things like the woman wiv' the big hat, *Indian Anna Jones*, or someone, and that *Times Team* lot on telly?" said Pincher Pete.

"That's what I said, archie-olo-jist. Now then, he was

coming regularly trying to get us criminals to learn stuff and get an interest so it would do us good. Well it's gonna do me some good, it's gonna get me rich! Apparently there are stories that somewhere on this river is a sunken Viking longboat."

"Sure it's not a Viking short boat? The river's quite narrow in places and it couldn't turn round," asked Pincher Pete.

"Don't think so, he said *longboat*," continued the boss, "it's a type of boat, anyway it's supposed to have gold on it, gold bracelet thingies."

"Who said it was here?" asked Pincher Pete, who prided himself on knowing lots about the Broads.

"Local legend," said the boss, opening another can of beer and throwing the ring pull out of open window, narrowly missing Teddy's head. Teddy watched it slip between the boat and the bank and disappear into the water.

Why do that? said Teddy to himself. *It will take decades for it to rust away, and it could do harm to the creatures that live in the river. You wouldn't throw rubbish around your home, so don't do it to the animals, birds and fishes' homes either. It's madness.*

Back inside the cruiser Pincher Pete was getting more interested. "Legend?" he repeated.

"Yes, a Viking funeral boat full of gold and the body of a local Viking leader. Set alight and sunk somewhere near here."

"How do we find it?" asked Pincher Pete.

"We don't. You do!" said the boss.

"I can't swim," replied Pincher Pete.

"The archo-algeric-ist person or whatever he is can," said the boss.

"Archaeologist," interrupted the smaller crook, pleased he'd worked out how to pronounce *archaeologist*.

"Don't be cheeky!" shouted the boss, and the smaller man shrank back.

"Yes the archaeolo-oo-gist," stumbled the boss. "Well he lives nearby and he might be *persuaded* to tell us where it is, because he thinks he knows. He also knows something else we need to get as well. Eggs."

"Oh we got some eggs – there were some in the old ladies' shopping," said Pincher Pete.

"No, eggs that are worth money," said the boss.

"Easter eggs?" said Pincher Pete.

"NO!" said the boss crossly.

"Viking eggs?" asked Pincher Pete desperately.

"NO! Now you are being stupid every knows Viking's didn't lay eggs," said the boss.

"Nor did the Romans neither," said he smaller friend.

"Give me strength," said the boss. "It's valuable eggs. What's rare around here?" he asked hopefully.

"Mountains," said Pincher Pete, "there are absolutely no mountains around here. They're really rare."

The boss took off his hat and hit Pincher Pete on the head with it.

"You stupid twit. Bitterns! They're rare. I have contacts that collect rare birds' eggs and they want some bitterns' eggs."

"Isn't that illegal?" said Pincher Pete.

"Course it's illegal, what we do is illegal, we make our living being illegal. I've never done a legal job in my life. We are criminals, get it?!"

"Oh yes yes," said Pincher Pete, "and where are the bitterns' eggs?"

"In the bitterns' nests," said the boss.

"And," added the smaller crook, "we're going to find them because the archaeologist who lives near here is a keen ornthao... oprna... orn... bird watcher too. We can persuade him to tell us where they are."

"How will we persuade him?" asked Pincher Pete, "Duff him up a bit?"

"No much more subtle than that," smiled the boss.

"Give him a wedgie?" asked Pincher Pete.

"Oh no much more subtle than that," added the smaller crook, "much more subtle."

"No," said the boss, "no we're going to be as subtle as a train crash. He lives alone; he used to be a professor at the university but has now retired and spends his time doing things to help other people and places. One of those sorts, we hate those sorts. Committee fund raising, probably runs the local neighbourhood watch as well. Bah. If he don't tell us and show us where the boat is, and where the eggs are, we're going to do something he will hate."

"What?" asked Pincher Pete.

"Our mate in the car has gone back to London to get some little friends, " laughed the second crook.

"We're going to – no you're going to – let them go free in the river here, if that archeo bird-watching do-gooder doesn't tell us where the stuff is, we're – no you're – going to let them go in the water."

"You won't have to because he will tell us as he'd hate for us to let our little friends go on the rampage," said the second crook.

"What or who are these little friends?" asked Pincher Pete.

"Coypu," said the boss. "Coypu, great big rats which once terrorised the area."

"Oh they were really nasty," said Pincher Pete slowly.

"Oh very. They absolutely destroy plants and vegetation. They eat their way through tons of stuff as they're about the biggest water rat you can find. They're what are called *non-native species.* That means they aren't natural to this area and they will cause mayhem if they get loose and breed. They were once quite a problem as they used to be farmed for their fur when people liked to wear dead animal skins as they thought it looked nice. Some escaped and caused big problems. They have lots and lots of babies very quickly. If we tell him we're going to let our friends go walkies, he'll tell us, you see."

"Oh I don't want to do that," said Pincher Pete. "I like nicking stuff and things but I don't want to do that."

"My little friend," said the boss his hands grabbing Pincher Pete's neck, "there's no going back. There's only one way out now, and you wouldn't like that."

Pincher Pete was frightened, he'd got in with a very bad lot and things were looking black.

Outside, Teddy gasped at what he'd heard and fell into the reeds as he lost his step trying to hear everything. The criminals on the stolen boat heard a rustling outside. The smaller crook rushed out with a large knife to see what was going on. Teddy crawled back through the reeds before he could be seen or caught.

"Must have been a bird or something," said the smaller crook as he went back inside.

And just to help Teddy, a friendly swallow watching from above, swooped down and flew over the stolen boat, making sure the gang had seen her so they wouldn't suspect there had been a bear listening to their conversation.

Teddy ran and climbed, crawled and rolled through the reeds and bushes until he got to solid fields and then sat down with his head in his hands. This was awful. The prospect of coypu returning to the Broads was hideous; it took years to get rid of them. They came from South America and that's where they should stay. Teddy needed help and needed it now, this gang were ruthless and the entire wildlife of the Broads would be at risk if they carried out their threat! He felt very alone and frightened.

CHAPTER SIX

Sick!

With the mid July sun flooding the pontoon with a promising morning light, Lucy and Alfie arrived back to *The Little Blue Boat*, tied snuggly to the safe wooden platform. They'd just returned from the wash block at the river centre where they'd stayed the night on the small yacht. Their dad had slept in a tent in the nearby camping area.

They'd left him to clear away the breakfast things back at his tent, and were heading off to Beccles and the next rendezvous point, their auntie's house by the riverside. There would be their forlorn and fed up brother, Sam, nursing his sprained ankle.

"Can I steer today?" asked eight-year-old Alfie hopefully, pulling on his lifejacket and doing it up.

"Bits of the route of course," replied his skipper sister, twelve-year-old Lucy, finishing putting her lifejacket on as well.

Trying to be fair, and to encourage her youngest brother to sail more, she told him to take the helm as she began to untie the mooring ropes. She had of course checked the tide which was gently beginning to run up river taking them in the direction they wanted to go. She also made sure there was no other river traffic in the way, and waited for two cruisers to pass before she started to undo the ropes. Their dad was watching from a short distance away, he didn't want to interfere but wanted to make sure they were safe and doing things properly.

Soon the small yacht was heading up the river, its main sail up and the small electric motor pushing them along. There wasn't enough wind yet to fill the jib sail and allow them to sail the entire journey but Lucy hoped the wind would pick up.

As they moved towards the centre of the river ahead of them, around the corner, moored by a thin strip of grassy bank, was a small motor cruiser with three men on board. They were all still asleep; they'd been up late drinking the night before. They too were heading for Beccles, but for very different reasons.

Without knowing it, Lucy and Alfie passed the spot where a small Able Sea Bear was dozing in the reeds. He'd had a restless night knowing what the evil Pincher Pete and his chums were up to. He had to find the Marsh Man and get help. The threat of the return of the dreaded coypu was hideous, too horrible to contemplate. Riverbanks destroyed, creatures made homeless, food chains disrupted.

As he stretched and brushed his fur he felt a puff of warm breath on his neck.

Oh what's this? said Teddy to himself, fearing the worst and wondering if he might become breakfast for some mysterious big cat or some other monster he'd never met but often had nightmares about.

"Don't eat me, I am very small and not very tasty…" he whimpered, squeezing his eyes tightly shut.

He needn't have worried.

"Hello small bear, can we help?" said the first creature.

"The Marsh Man has asked us to look out for you," said the second.

Teddy turned round to see two nervous looking animals. "You're deer," said Teddy.

"Chinese water deer," said the first deer. "But we aren't really Chinese."

"No," said the second one, "we're not made of water either! Our ancestors came from Asia but our species has lived here since the nineteenth century."

The bear smiled. The two deer were a little bigger than a large dog and a lovely light brown-ish colour.

"Well it's nice to see you," said Teddy.

"Please, do climb on one of our backs and we'll take you to find the Marsh Man."

"Well thank you," said the Able Sea Bear and, as the first deer bent down to allow the bear to get a grip, Teddy pulled himself onto the graceful animal's back.

"I hope I'm not too heavy for you," said the bear, grateful for the lift.

"Not at all," replied the deer, standing up to its full height. "I can manage; you're only a small bear after all." With that, the two deer, with Able Sea Bear Teddy on one of their backs, headed off inland over the meadows.

*

"Can you pull the jib sheet any tighter?" asked Alfie, looking at the sails, and trying to get the most speed out of the light wind.

"It's pretty tight," replied Lucy, feeling the tension on the thin rope tied firmly around a cleat on the deck. *The Little Blue Boat* was making its way up the Waveney. Lucy and Alfie were hoping to get to Beccles before tea time to moor up at their aunt's house, which had a narrow garden stretching down to the riverbank itself with enough room for a small boat to tie to. Waiting for them would be their brother, Sam, nursing his sprained ankle. Their dad had said he would be there to meet them and help them plan the next part of their – now altered – voyage.

The curves and bends on the wandering River Waveney took the two children and *The Little Blue Boat* past fields, trees and water meadows, all under a big open sky. Lucy smiled as she felt the wind tug the small sails of the little yacht. She knew she wanted to explore, to learn and to enjoy boats and the water. There were seas and oceans out there waiting to be sailed and conquered as our ancestors had done before in lives gone by. One day she wanted to sail big yachts and feel big waves and strong winds. It was in her blood and every part of her eager young self. Birds flew by, fish swam under the waves. She loved it, and the world felt good.

*

Waking up, late and hungover, Pincher Pete crawled out from under a blanket on a side berth in the stolen motor cruiser. He went ashore to have a wee. The little boat toilet had been bunged up with toilet paper and stank of sick. The three thieves had drunk beer the night before; and whiskey; and brandy; and more beer. They'd gone through the boat's lockers and found some drink which the owner's had kept on board and they'd drunk the lot.

The smaller of the two men who Pincher Pete was helping had been sick, very sick. It was everywhere and was smelly. The two gangsters hadn't realised you shouldn't put paper down boat toilets. The pipework is so small it easily blocks up. Also it's not at all nice to have it floating around the water. Most boats have a 'holding tank' where stuff from the toilet goes in to and is kept until it's emptied either at out at sea or by pumping it out in a special place. Paper and stuff like that is put into a bin, or into bags and then in a bin. These two didn't know and wouldn't listen even if Pincher Pete had told them. It was a horrid mess.

Pincher Pete held his head and yawned. He felt for a cigarette in his pocket but he'd run out. If the others had got any he'd be in trouble. Nicotine, the drug that's in cigarettes, is so addictive that if you don't keep taking it you feel really horrid. It can drain you of money, your health and ultimately your life itself. Pincher Pete was a wreck. He heard his two friends, the gangsters in the boat, shouting at each other because of the toilet. Then the boss, the biggest and nastiest of the two, came out of the cabin and said four words Pincher was dreading.

"Pete, clean the bog."

When Pincher Pete froze, motionless, reeling in horror at the prospect, the big man climbed out of the boat and stood in front of him on the riverbank. He leaned in close to Pincher Pete's face and said in a low, frightening voice: "Clean the bog. Now!"

*

Walking gently through the morning's soft sunshine, were the two Chinese water deer with Able Sea Bear Teddy on one of their backs.

"Have you lived around here long?" asked the small bear, hanging on to the deer's neck as he was transported through the water meadow.

"We were born close to here," said the deer carrying him.

"Our ancestors were immigrants. Many were brought for zoos and wildlife parks, some of them escaped and some were released and now live in small groups here."

"Do the locals mind?" asked the Able Sea Bear.

"No no," said the other deer, "we all get on and help each other."

"That's nice," replied the bear.

"Yes many birds and animals migrate and move around you know," said the first deer.

"It's some humans that seem to have problems with other humans moving around. Odd really as most of the people who live around here can trace their ancestors back to other parts of Europe."

"I wonder where the Marsh Man is from?" mused the Able Sea Bear. "Do you know where we will find him?"

"Not sure," replied the deer carrying him, "he knows you need to see him urgently. I'm sure we'll see him soon."

"Your special canoe is waiting for you Teddy," said

the second deer and turned to the river. There tied to a small tree branch was the little canoe which Teddy had been given earlier, and which he was plucked from by the holidaymakers on the River Yare.

"Ah my little log!" said Teddy, pleased to see the small lump of wood, carefully carved out to be able to be paddled but without looking too obvious.

Teddy climbed off the small deer's back as it bent down to be closer to the ground. The deer didn't want the Able Sea Bear to fall. The bear said his goodbyes, and patted each of the deer on their noses to say thank you, then climbed on to the canoe, checking his lifejacket was still firmly fixed, which it was.

Lucy and Alfie were on *The Little Blue Boat* a little way behind Teddy and his canoe, but didn't know.

Behind them was Pincher Pete and the two gangsters in the stolen motor cruiser, just about to set off from the bank after eating some dry bread and waiting for poor old Pincher Pete to clean the loo.

"Ugh this is HORRIBLE," said Pincher Pete, his hands in the toilet pulling out paper, with the stink of sick all around him. "I hate the smell of SICK!" he said, holding his nose with one hand.

"Hurry up!" shouted the boss of the gang, "I want to go!"

"Oh yuk," said Pete, *I'll never get involved with bad men again*, he said to himself.

Oh but he would, in a few years he would do something very, very bad, and threaten the entire Broads system, but that is in the future.

Soon the three thieves were getting ready to leave. They didn't know if the boat had yet been reported as being stolen. Its owners were away out of the country, but just to be sure, and to make it harder for the Navigation Rangers to find them, they had scratched the name of the boat off the bow and stern – that's the front and back in boat language. They'd also altered the registration number on the boat with a black marker pen by changing some numbers.

The cruiser's engine started with a cough and a puff of exhaust. The bad guys' boat set off as fast as it could but with Pincher Pete at the wheel ready to slow down the second another boat came into view just in case it was the Rangers. They were behind *The Little Blue Boat* with Lucy and Alfie on board and behind the Able Sea Bear, but Lucy and Alfie were sailing slowly, and Teddy was paddling. If Pincher Pete and the gang caught up with them it could end in disaster. Pincher Pete was still determined to get his revenge on *The Little Blue Boat* and Able Sea Bear Teddy, as it was while stealing the boat that he'd been arrested and thrown in jail the year before.

The kingfisher flying over the river suddenly realised the gang's cruiser would soon catch them up.

Alfie was now at the helm steering *The Little Blue Boat*, Lucy had brought up some biscuits and orange juice from inside the small cabin. She'd picked up her brother's sleeping bag which had fallen from the small berth because the boat had tipped a few times as they sailed the river.

They had just seen the fields on the right – or starboard side – turn to woodland and the ground get a little higher. They were closing on Beccles but still had a way to go. Just ahead of them a small bear on a small piece of wood paddled into the riverbank by the trees. The bear had no idea the children or his beloved *Little Blue Boat* was so close. The children had no idea either or they would have met up and had a wonderful reunion. That, though, would have to wait.

The Able Sea Bear had been paddling for fifteen minutes when he saw the familiar figure of the Marsh Man at the side of the river. He held his old paddle high in the air and waved. Teddy felt very relived but he was worried that this time even the Marsh Man couldn't stop the evil Pincher Pete's plans. He tried a smile, but was so worried he was frowning and sad.

CHAPTER SEVEN

Vikings!

Lucy took the tiller – that's the wooden stick that you steer a boat with. She guided the small yacht along the river, passing the row of moored boats on the port side (that's the left side) of the riverbank. The girl skipper started the electric motor and asked Alfie to take the sails down. She then stopped the boat on the special bit of quayside just before the bridge, which is reserved for yachts to take down their masts. When the boat had stopped, Alfie went ashore and tied the front and rear ropes around the little wooden mooring posts along the edge of the wooden quay so that the boat would be safely moored.

Lucy moved forward and uncoupled the boom – that's the piece of metal which goes at the bottom of the mast for the sail to attach to – and put it on the top of the deck. She then caught the mast as Alfie lowered it down after untying the piece of rope that held it to the very front of the boat. Alfie then tied the mast and boom together and to the top of the deck to make sure it couldn't fall off, and all the ropes were tied up or tucked away. The boat was then ready to carry on with its journey under the bridge. It's always best to allow plenty of time to lower your mast to go under bridges, you may not be able to stop in time if there's a current, or if there's nowhere close to a bridge to moor up and drop the mast. They'd been followed by a kingfisher, dipping and darting along the riverbank, hiding between branches and reeds, watching their every move.

With the mast down, they went under the bridge that spanned the river and on into Beccles. To the left of them, the port side, were the moorings and public quayside with a little café and small shop next to the Harbour Master's office. The Harbour Master is in charge of the harbour or port and tells boats where they should moor up, often helping where he, or she, can.

They then went under the second bridge and pretty houses appeared along the left-hand side of the river, this was Beccles, an old and picturesque market town. Standing on a small strip of land where a long thin garden met the river was Sam, waving, his poorly ankle still in a bandage. Next to him were the children's dad and their aunty who lived in the house by the river, where they would be staying the night. There was just enough room for *The Little Blue Boat* to tie up on the tiny strip of riverbank which was part of the garden.

Just behind them, coming under the bridge, were Pincher Pete and the two gangsters in the stolen motor cruiser. Pincher Pete saw *The Little Blue Boat* which had just stopped by the garden's quay heading. He squinted as he watched three children hug each other and their dad. He knew it was the boat he had stolen a year ago and the boat where the nasty little bear had bitten him on the bum and no one had believed him.

"I'll get that boat!" he snarled.

"Not yet you won't," said the bigger of the two bad men, adding, "you keep going, we've got a job to do."

Pincher Pete reluctantly drove the small motor cruiser onwards but as he passed *The Little Blue Boat* and its happy crew, he said, "I must just *accidently* bash into them!" and turned the wheel. As he did, the kingfisher watching from above, swooped down and knocked the hat off the biggest bad guy. It fell into the water.

"MY HAT! MY HAT! Get it Pincher Pete or you're in trouble!" he growled menacingly.

Under the water a grass snake swam underneath the hat, popping his head up in the dark space as the hat floated along, and then propelled it along the river away from where *The Little Blue Boat* was moored up.

"Chase that hat!" shouted the boss bad man to the worried Pincher Pete.

They slowed the cruiser down, and circled around so the smallest of the gang members could lean over the edge of the boat, reach over and hook the hat up in a fishing net. The snake, having played his part, smiled and swam off. The kingfisher knew they had distracted the gang away from *The Little Blue Boat*, but they knew there was evil to come.

*

In the reeds the Marsh Man bent down and picked up the small, frightened little bear.

"My little friend," said the Marsh Man smiling, his old gnarled fingers holding the Able Sea Bear gently, "How are you? And what a journey you've made to find me!"

"It's Pincher Pete," said the bear quietly. "I have heard their terrible plans," he continued.

"Tell me more," said the Marsh Man, moving to a fallen branch and sitting down with the bear beside him, while the otter swam backwards and forwards along the bank keeping watch.

"There's some Viking gold in a sunken boat," said Teddy.

"Ah yes," nodded the Marsh Man, "I wondered how long it would be for that to be found again."

"Again? Found again?" said Teddy surprised.

"Mmmm yes," nodded the Marsh Man. "It's been there since the Vikings brought their longboats up these rivers centuries ago. They didn't all have funny hats with horns you know, that's what people added to the myths of the Vikings a few hundred years ago."

"Really?" said the bear interested. "How do you know?"

"Well," said the Marsh Man as if he were about to say something very important, "Well…" then he stopped.

"You weren't there? You're not THAT old… are you?" asked Teddy, shocked by the thought.

"Let's just say," replied the Marsh Man, "let's just say I have been around for long enough to know a lot of things."

"Do you know where the gold is?" asked the bear.

"Of course, it's on the river bed near Burgh St Peter on the River Waveney."

"Why haven't you dug it up? Recovered it?" asked the bear.

"I have no need of gold. I want it to go to the right place, that's a museum, when the right person can find it and take it there," said the Marsh Man firmly.

"Well," said Teddy, "these three bad men are going to force a poor archy… achey… arch-holo-gist."

"Archaeologist?" asked the Marsh Man, "Is that what you mean? Someone who researches the past, and the way we lived in the past?"

"Yes, that's him," said Teddy. "Well they're going to force him to tell them where it is, AND to tell them where the bitterns' nests are so they can steal the eggs!"

"That cannot be allowed," said the Marsh Man firmly.

"But they are threatening to release coypu."

The Marsh Man stood up, threw back his head and looked stern. "That would be terrible. Terrible. The poor coypu aren't to blame, it's in their nature, but they destroyed riverbanks, miles of them in the past and tons of vegetation. Sadly they had to be killed off. If they come back they will threaten the entire Broads and the rivers beyond."

*

"Right," said the boss bad man, "I think the house should be up on the hill in that street round the corner."

It was just getting dark. Pincher Pete had steered the stolen cruiser along the River Waveney, which had slowly become narrower and in many ways prettier, as they had left Beccles and headed towards the end of navigation, which was at Geldeston Locks. The Locks is a nice pub where the river is crossed by a small footbridge. There's a small ferry which runs between here and Beccles carrying tourists. That was during the day, this was nearly night, and the three bad guys with Pincher Pete at the front, walked sheepishly past the pub, having tied up by the quayside, and walked into the car park. A dark car put on its lights and the passenger door was pushed open by the driver inside. It was the third member of the gang who Pincher Pete was helping.

"Have you got the coypu?" asked the boss.

"Yup," replied the voice from inside the car. "All tucked up in their cage in that ruined cottage we found.

"The one I found," said Pincher Pete, taking the credit for helping them.

"Let's go, quick," said the boss.

The three got into the car and the driver gently pulled away so as not to attract attention. However, they had been seen by a bat, which quickly darted off to pass the message on.

The archaeologist was at home. He was alone; his children were grown up and had left home. His wife had gone to visit her sister who lived in the Canary Islands on Fuerteventura. She was always going on about how nice it must be to live there but the archaeologist liked living at Geldeston. He loved the Broads, the East Anglian coast with its crumbing cliffs and sandy beaches, its marshes and sand dunes. He had been a teacher at the university and now spent his time teaching prisoners at a nearby jail, helping to improve their education. He also liked to help look after the birds and the rivers.

He had been researching old parish records and reports of a Viking longboat, the remains of which had been found back in the 1800s. He thought he knew where it must be and hoped to organise a 'dig', or rather an underwater search for it, if he could get permission of course. He was sure there was a gold torque there as well, which is a beautiful, circular necklace made of twisted strands of gold wire. There were old reports of one having been seen but never brought to the surface, because it had been protected by a strange old man. He would give it to the museum if he found it. He had also been watching the bitterns' nest, knowing there were precious eggs there, the baby birds inside slowly growing beneath the protective shell. There were only a few bitterns on the Broads and it was vital to help them survive. As we know, the bitterns are the most respected birds on the Broads and every month they hold the Bittern Council on the secret broad where nobody knows, except the Marsh Man and he never tells. The archaeologist had precious knowledge. Knowledge he had shared in his teaching in the prison, hoping to inspire the convicts in the jail, sadly it had only inspired one of them to want to steal both the gold and the eggs.

It was getting dark and he was watching a programme on TV. There was a knock at the door.

Oh who's that? he wondered and got up to answer the door. He switched on the outside light that shone above the front door of his cottage. He saw the shape of a man, a man wearing a hat.

*

"Thanks Aunty," said Lucy, "that was great." The three children and their dad had just eaten one of Auntie's famous quiches with new potatoes and baked beans.

"So Sam," said the children's father, "you've been very patient with that poor ankle of yours. I'm sure you can have a little trip on *The Little Blue Boat*, perhaps up the river to the Geldeston Locks and back, so long as you don't get it wet or put any pressure on it."

"Thanks Dad!" said Sam, relieved that at last he'd be able to join his brother and sister for some of the journey.

"I'll wait here for you and see you when you get back," said his dad.

After they'd eaten they watched TV. Lucy walked down to check the boat, which was sitting quietly tied to the piece of quay heading at the bottom of her aunt's garden. She looked up; the moon was barely visible. She sat on the small yacht after checking the mooring lines and making sure the hatches were closed.

I wonder where Teddy is? she said to herself. A bat flew past, dipping and swerving as it went. It headed off across the fields opposite the house. Lucy turned to go back, and stopped for a moment. She heard the sound of a small motor cruiser coming down the river. As it passed she was sure she could hear muffled shouts. She turned and went back into the house, the smell of a summer evening was in the air.

The cruiser passed under the bridge and headed towards Burgh St Peter, where the sunken Viking longboat lay under the water, undisturbed for centuries, with its valuable ancient treasure.

CHAPTER EIGHT

Forced!

The sea was getting rough. *The Little Blue Boat* with Lucy at the helm was heading towards the entrance in the sea wall, which protected Lowestoft Harbour. As the small yacht went out the full force of the current became clear. Powerful waves pushed the boat south, and despite the electric outboard being on full power Lucy had little control. The sails were up too and soon filled with the gusts of wind. Her two brothers held the jib sheets, and held on.

Before long Lowestoft had gone, the boat was being pushed along at the mercy of the wind and the waves. Lucy had no control. The waves got bigger. Much bigger, soon they were taller than the boat itself and waves were crashing over the deck and soaking the three children to the skin.

"I'm cold!" shouted Sam

"Me too," echoed his brother, looking worried.

Lucy was scared. Soon the water was spilling in to the floor of the cabin; Lucy looked down and saw how much the boat was filling up.

"Put the washboards on NOW!" she screamed. The washboards are the two wooden doors which cover the hatch to the cockpit and keep water out. But it was too late. As Sam picked them up a wave knocked them out of his hand and they went overboard into the choppy, racing, grey, angry sea. A seagull flew above desperate to help but knew it couldn't.

More water came into the small yacht, Lucy turn the boat round but picked the wrong moment. The wave crashed over the boat, the water inside tipped to one side, and the weight of the water inside and outside forced the boat to turn over. The three children went under the water with the boat, which filled with water and started to sink.

Lucy's face was wet.

She woke up. It had been a nightmare, and in her thrashing about she had knocked over a glass of water onto her hair and pillow.

"You're dreaming Lucy!" said Sam, half asleep; having been woken up by his sister's mumbling cries.

"I've been dreaming too!" said Alfie. "I was dreaming of having a bath in liquid chocolate! Instead of pulling the plug out I drank it all!"

"You pig!" laughed Sam. "I was dreaming," he added thoughtfully, "of Able Sea Bear Teddy, I dreamt he was OK and looking for us, and he was talking!"

"Don't be silly," said Lucy, "teddy bears can't talk."

"Of course," said Sam. "That would be silly... wouldn't it?"

The children fell back to sleep in the spare room of their aunt's house on the riverbank in Beccles. Lucy realised that if she ever wanted to go to sea she would have to be qualified first; she would need to learn how to navigate tides and currents and would only take a very small boat out in perfect conditions. She would need a radio, flares and life-lines to strap herself and her crew to the boat itself so they couldn't be washed overboard. She realised you can never underestimate the power of the waves and the sea.

*

The driver of the gang's car was crawling along a little lane. He was trespassing, as this wasn't a public road. It was dark. The road was a bumpy track, just mud and a few bricks for a base. The driver had turned off the lights and was crawling along slowly using a map reference in his sat nav. He bounced around as the car's wheels went in and out of bumps and holes.

The car stopped and the shadowy figure of the driver got out. Undoing the lid of the boot he heard a scuffle, inside the boot of the car was a cage, in the cage were three large, rat-like creatures. Coypu. They were frightened and hungry. The driver picked up the cage and put it on a little trolley, which he pulled out of the boot from next to the cage. He dragged the trolley with the cage on top, over the rough track and through the marsh, until he had to pick up the cage and move it through the scrub.

"Cor this is heavy," he said, "I hate these things, still if they get out they'll tear their way through the undergrowth and destroy the riverbanks so nothing else can live there."

Coypu eat the stems of plants leaving most of it to die and go to waste. They also have lots of babies, very quickly and dig big holes in the riverbanks.

The driver dragged the cage through the wet undergrowth. He'd been given a map by Pincher Pete a few weeks before. He was at the south side of the River Waveney near Oulton Broad. Here the river has a few inlets which were dug out to be sort of laybys for the old trading wherries, they were the big barge-like boats which worked the rivers and broads before the railways. They carried coal, wood, grain and other stuff between the towns, farms and the seas. These laybys were places they could stop for a while.

Behind these inlets was a stream called Sutton's Dyke. This was where the driver was heading. At the end of the dyke where it meets the river, he put down the cage, pulled a torch from his pocket and turned it on, searching with the pale yellow light for a plank of wood which Pincher Pete had put there weeks before. He would use this to get across the dyke. As an owl watched he picked up the damp piece of wood and laid it across the narrow dyke. Picking up the cage he carefully went across the plank to the other side. There in the trees was the small, old, broken down remains of a cottage. Just three walls and a small part of the roof remained. It was hidden from view and this is where he would keep the coypu until he got the phone call to release them.

He'd got them from Dirty Dodgy Darren who'd driven them back from Italy, hidden under a blanket in his van behind a load of engines he'd brought back to sell. Dirty Dodgy Darren had handed over the coypu the day before he was arrested for smuggling stolen engines.

The driver hunched up in the corner of the tumbled down building. He hoped people would think the car had been left by someone going for a walk. Besides, he knew it would only be for a few days at the most. He had a few sandwiches with him as well as some beer and a flask of coffee; he would be OK for a while. He hadn't, though, brought anything for the coypu, which were very hungry and clearly upset. The owl watched silently, shaking its head from side to side, thinking the driver was a very horrible man.

*

Dawn began to break, the early summer sun rising across the Broads. The fresh morning mist hovered above the ground, making the trees and reeds look mysterious and magical. The birds woke first, followed by the animals and then the fish. The insects waited until the sun warmed their wings before taking to the air.

Half sitting, half lying against an old willow tree, its yellowish thin branches covering him like a canopy, Able Sea Bear Teddy started to wake. He flexed his paws and yawned. Opening his eyes he noticed that the Marsh Man had gone. Sitting there was a water vole, washing its mouth and nose with its paws.

"Ah you're awake?" said the vole. "I have a message from, er, who was it from?"

"The Marsh Man?" enquired Teddy.

"Yes that's him, of course," the vole coughed. "He went off last night for an urgent meeting with the Bittern Council. He said to tell you an emergency has been declared across the Broads. All the birds are in a right flap. Well a left flap too I suppose otherwise they'd fly round and round in circles and get nowhere!" the vole laughed. "Sorry, it is serious, yes, the birds are in a flap," he sniggered, "the fish are in a flop and the sheep are in a flock! Ha ha, no sorry, the otters are anxious, the deer are desperate, and the bitterns are blooming furious. Your orders are to wait for a peregrine falcon. They are the fastest birds around these parts, and some of them are living in Norwich at the cathedral. Urgent messages have been tweeted by the other birds to scramble the fastest falcon to come and meet up here, soon."

"Oh dear," said Teddy, "another fast flight, I do get a little air sick you know."

"Well it IS an emergency," said the vole, who turned his head back and forth and said, "I'm off, be careful," and scurried away squeaking.

"Bye," said the bear and held his head in his paws wondering what would happen next.

*

The city of Norwich with its medieval streets, beautiful buildings and bustling market was beginning to bubble into life. Buses stopped and people got off ready to go to work in offices and shops, hospitals and hairdressers. Tourists woke in hotels and in the cruisers moored alongside the quay on the river near the railway station at the Norwich Yacht Station.

Standing proud above the city was the cathedral spire, said to be the second tallest spire in England. On a ledge on its tranquil and safe stonework the peregrine falcons were watching the bustle below. One twitched and listened to a passing swallow. He was tweeting the news about the emergency and about Teddy waiting on the riverbank. The peregrines shook their feathers and the strongest flyer looked at the sky to check the weather, looked around and flapped its powerful wings. It took to the air with a whoosh and a graceful glide. It headed towards the river.

*

Teddy heard a *rat tat tatting* noise and got up quickly, worried that something or someone was about to pounce on him or even eat him!

There in the branches of the next tree was a strange bird pecking the wood.

"Er who or what are you?" asked Teddy.

"Oh sorry, yes, a bit noisy I know. I'm a woodpecker," replied the woodpecker.

"Wood picker?" said Teddy confused, "You'll never pick up all that wood, your beak isn't big enough, that's a whole tree you know."

"Yes *rat tat tat*," said the woodpecker, "yes I know, no I am a woodPECKER: I peck wood."

"Well," said Teddy, "everyone needs a hobby I suppose."

"No it's not a hobby!" said the woodpecker, flying down to sit beside Teddy. "I do it to pick up bugs."

"Oh that's dangerous," replied Teddy shaking his head. "My aunty picked up a bug and she was ill for ages."

"Not that sort of bug!" said the woodpecker, shaking its greyish feathers with their white stripes. Its pretty head with a flash of crimson red on the top of it was glinting in the morning sun. "In fact, I'm a lesser-spotted woodpecker. I'm a bit less common than my cousins the green woodpeckers or the great spotted woodpeckers. I'm also a boy, and have a brighter red bit on the top of my head. It looks rather fetching don't you think? I catch bugs to eat, wood boring bugs; you know, critters that burrow into old trees and fallen wood. Some of my cousins love ants, really love ants. I thought you said you had an ant-y not aunty, if you had an ant-y I would probably consider eating her as well!"

"You wouldn't like to eat my aunt, she's not an ant she's a rather old crusty teddy bear."

"Well that's good then. Ah there's some larvae in that tree branch, sorry must dash, bye."

With that the woodpecker flew up to the tree and began pecking again. *Rat tat tat, rat tat tat.*

"Oh dear," said the Able Sea Bear, "it's going to be a noisy morning."

*

The peregrine falcon swooped low and flew fast. Soon he was looking for the bear, scouring the riverbank, and then he spotted him, walking around under the willow tree. The falcon checked he was clear for landing and whizzed through the branches like a bolt of lightning. The bear squealed and was almost scared out of his fur.

*

Along the river the stolen brown cruiser was stopping near Burgh St Peter; half hiding in a small dyke to reduce the risk of being seen by passing boats.

*

In Beccles the three children were on *The Little Blue Boat* heading, they thought, to Geldeston Locks.

They were wrong. Waiting for them along the riverbank by the old Beccles Lido swimming pool was the Marsh Man. He was waving his old paddle and calling for them to stop. He had an urgent message, but would they listen?

CHAPTER NINE

Gold!

"Thanks Lucy," said Sam, taking the helm for the first time. The morning sun was bathing the pretty houses with soft morning light. Sam had spent the last few days at his aunt's house with his dad after spraining his ankle, waiting for his chance to go back on *The Little Blue Boat*, and now it had come.

They were heading upstream, up to the end of navigation at Geldeston Locks, a lovely little voyage and they hoped to be able to sail for most of the way. They started off with the little electric motor purring away as they headed off into the sunny morning. Soon the houses wood give way to open countryside then the tree-lined bank of the river as it meandered inland. They saw the tower of St Michael's Church on the higher ground in the town. It has three clock faces and one side blank.

"Auntie told me," said Alfie, "that when it was built the clocks were designed only to be seen on the three sides facing the county of Suffolk, which is the county Beccles is in, and so the side of the tower facing the county of Norfolk, which is on the other side of the river, was blank."

"Why?" asked Sam.

"It was said," replied his brother, "that Suffolk people wouldn't even give Norfolk people the time of day."

"I don't understand," said Sam.

"Well," said Lucy, "it means there was a lot of rivalry between the two counties so they wouldn't help each other."

"That's sad," said Sam. "It makes sense to join up to help each other and share things. Who's that waving at us?" asked Sam pointing to a large figure of a man holding a paddle in the air, standing on the edge of the river near the Beccles Lido – that's the outdoor swimming pool.

"That's the man who waved us to safety on Breydon Water," said Lucy, "he told us to moor up on the old landing stage when we were lost. Let's see what he wants. It looks urgent."

"Hello!" called the Marsh Man, watching Sam steer the small yacht perfectly against the little quay side in front of the lido. Lucy threw the ropes for the Marsh Man to catch and he held the boat still. "Sorry to stop you, but there's a problem," he said, "you have to go back under the bridge as fast as you can, and go to Burgh St Peter. There you will find your friend Able Sea Bear Teddy."

"What!" said Alfie.

"You've seen Teddy?!" shrieked Sam.

"Where has he been, is he OK?" asked Lucy.

"Teddy is OK, he's been, um lost at sea, or rather lost

in the river for a bit but, the important thing is, there's a friend of the Broads who's in trouble, he's an archaeologist who knows where a sunken Viking longboat is."

"Is their treasure on it? Maybe swords?" asked Sam, interrupting.

"Cheese?" said Alfie not thinking.

"Bones?" asked Lucy.

"No, gold," said the Marsh Man, "but the archaeologist is being forced to show a gang of bad men led by the horrible Pincher Pete where the gold is."

"Oh no," said Lucy.

"It's worse than that," said the Marsh Man gravely, "they are also planning to steal the bitterns' eggs."

"Why?" asked Alfie.

"To sell them to other bad people who collect birds' eggs," replied the Marsh Man.

"We must stop them. Why don't we tell the Rangers or the police?" asked Alfie.

"We will," said the Marsh Man, "but there's something else as well, the gang are threatening to release something called coypu into the rivers. They are a sort of giant rat, and they will do terrible damage to the environment. The problem is," said the Marsh Man, "I don't yet know where the coypu are being kept. If we tell everyone now they'll launch a major operation which will spread fear and panic among all the creatures that live on the Broads. We can stop this ourselves, I've done it before. We also need to know which bitterns' nest they are going to target. We will tell the Rangers very soon but there's no time right now and we must let the animals and birds try to sort it out first." The Marsh Man turned *The Little Blue Boat* around and pushed it off back towards Beccles bridge in the direction of Burgh St Peter where the gold was, and where the gang were heading.

"Come on," said Lucy, taking the helm from her brother. "Let's get the mast down again while we're on the move so we can go under the bridge quickly, and let's turn up the engine to the speed limit to get there as soon as we can."

"What about Dad? He's expecting us at Geldeston?" said Sam.

"I know, use the mobile phone in the cabin to ring him and say we've stopped off on the riverbank to watch birds," said Lucy.

"OK," said Sam and went to phone their dad.

Soon they were heading away from Beccles and back on the open river.

"Come on *Little Blue Boat*, as fast as you can," said Alfie "I want to see Teddy again."

"Put the mast up then," said Lucy, "there's a good wind coming and we can sail faster than we can motor!"

The kingfisher flew above the boat and watched a fast moving peregrine falcon swoop out of the sky and land further up the riverbank, then take off again with a small bear on its back.

*

Near Burgh St Peter the archaeologist was wading in the water in his bare feet and pants. The gang had forced him to go looking for the gold treasure. He'd been kept in the cabin for ages as they wanted to wait for the morning river traffic to move through before looking.

"It's not the way to do a dig, to search for ancient

relics," he pleaded. "We'll never find it like this; the water is being stirred up."

"Just keep looking!" barked the boss of the gang.

The archaeologist was looking where he thought it was, from his research, but he could find nothing. He was wading down the remains of a small dyke off the riverbank, now silted up; then his foot kicked against a piece of wood, an old piece of curved, carved wood. He bent down and felt it.

"Wow!" he gasped. "This could be part of a real Viking longboat!"

As he did *The Little Blue Boat* came sailing round the corner. The children dropped the sails and slowed the boat.

"Where's our Teddy?" demanded Alfie, waving a boat hook.

"Free that archaeologist!" screamed Lucy.

"We're on to you," said Sam, taking the tiller.

"It's that horrid little boat!" shouted Pincher Pete.

"Right!" shouted the boss and pulled a mobile phone from his pocket. "You lot better stay away or I'll press 'send' and this text will tell my driver to release the coypu and you wouldn't want that!"

He turned to the archaeologist and said, "Find the gold NOW or I'll send the text!"

"I can't just find the gold, it could be under the mud, it might not even be here!" said the archaeologist, bending over in the water desperately searching the edge of the mud with his hands.

Then a voice boomed out from the reeds.

"Is THIS what you're looking for?!" said the Marsh Man and raised his right hand. In it was a bright shining gold torque, glinting in the sunshine.

"Hand it over NOW!" shrieked the boss.

"Once you promise not to release the coypu. I now know where they are, the owl has just told me! And, when you release the archaeologist and those children."

"NOW or I text! You're too late old man, the archaeologist has already told me where the eggs are, he's drawn us a map, so you'd better go away after you've given me the torque," said the boss grinning.

Above the river travelling very, very fast, Teddy was clinging on to the peregrine falcon.

I've never gone this fast! said Teddy to himself. *My ears are being pushed back and my fur is being parted in all the wrong ways by the force of the wind. We're so high I can see half of the Broad from up here, and the North Sea as well! Agh the bird is diving down towards those boats. Oh! There's the children, and Pincher Pete!*

The Marsh Man threw the golden torque towards the boss who tried to grab it, but he missed. As it fell they all heard a yell in the sky. A small Able Sea Bear fell from a peregrine falcon and landed on the boss's arm, knocking the phone out of his hand. It fell into the water with a loud, sad *plop*.

The torque was just about to hit the water too when the falcon swooped down and grabbed it in its beak. He flew upwards and away. The phone hit the water and suddenly bounced up again, knocked into the air by the nose of the otter. It landed further along the river and was bounced by another otter. They passed it between them and disappeared into the riverbank's reeds.

"That's Teddy!" shouted Sam.

"How did he get up there in the sky?" asked Alfie.

"The bird might have found him and was taking him back to use him to build his nest with, he has soft fur."

"Teddy! Used as nesting material?" said Alfie, upset.

"We'll get him back, he's on that cruiser with the bad men, " said Sam.

In all the excitement no one noticed Teddy crawl into the cruiser's cabin and hide. The boss grabbed another phone from his colleague and laughed.

"You really think we'd have just one phone?! Stay away or we set the coypu free!"

The stolen cruiser had powered up its engine and was roaring off along the river as fast as it could.

Just then the sky became very dark, thick clouds appeared and thunder started.

"It's that wind, I thought it was bringing a weather front in," said Lucy.

The Marsh Man said, "They are heading for the marshes near Surlingham on the River Yare. I'm going to find the coypu. Go and get help as soon as you can." He disappeared into the reeds.

As they turned to follow the stolen cruiser, the rain started falling.

"We must rescue Teddy!" said Alfie.

"We'll follow that boat," said Sam, pulling out the jib sail.

Lucy started the engine.

Sam said, "We must tell Dad we're going after Teddy. He'll understand, tell him we're heading towards Surlingham, and I'll ask him to call the Rangers and the police."

He picked up the phone but there was no signal. They'd have to wait to call for help.

The three children chased after the bad gang in the stolen cruiser. Pincher Pete had to keep his speed down otherwise they would draw attention to them and they couldn't risk that. They'd lost the torque but they could still steal the eggs. They'd been promised a good price for them so they knew they mustn't fail.

After a while, the boss picked up the phone and dialled the driver who was still waiting in the ruined remains of the cottage near Outlon Broad. "Hello it's me. Listen. I'm going to do it. Let the coypu loose. NOW."

"Right-oh boss," the driver said, and turned off his phone. He went to the cage and dragged it to the end of the cottage wall. He undid the catch and opened the door on the metal cage. The three hungry coypu crawled out and started eating. He packed up his stuff and thought about leaving. As he did he watched the three rodents slither across the scrub and slip into the River Waveney. He had done a terrible thing.

Just as he started to walk back along the plank to go back to his car on the other side of the dyke, he saw the shape of a large man with a paddle appear on the other side.

"Hello mate," said the driver smiling.

"You're no mate of mine or the Broads, you're going to jail," said the Marsh Man.

"Oh am I?" said the driver, and put his fists up. "I was a boxer, and a night club bouncer, do you really think an old man like you can stop me!" he sneered.

The Marsh Man suddenly swooped low and swung his paddle around, knocking the driver behind his knees. The driver gasped and fell backwards into the dyke.

"Right old man," he said, "you're going to regret that, when I get out of here."

"When you get out of here you're going to jail!" said the Marsh Man, and added, "But you've still got to get out of there first."

"That won't be difficult," said the driver, but then he saw a swirling in the water – there were eels everywhere on one side of him. He turned around and there were more slithering things in the water, grass snakes.

"Agh they're horrid get them away!" shrieked the driver, falling back into the muddy dyke.

"Not till my friends get here," replied the Marsh Man.

"But they're going up my trousers!" screamed the driver.

"Yes," said the Marsh Man, "that's because I told them to."

The snakes swam to the back of the driver's trousers and hooked their forked tongues around the top of his pants.

"Ever been given a wedgie by snakes before?" asked the Marsh Man, stepping over the plank bridge.

"OOOH HHHH OOOOOH!" shouted the driver as the snakes pulled harder and the eels swam up and down his trouser legs, tickling his legs with their slimy bodies. "OOOOHHHH!"

They say his cries could be heard all the way to Somerleyton.

The Marsh Man crossed the bridge and waded and walked through the undergrowth to the old wherry layby off the main river. At the end were the three coypu, sitting in the water having just eaten a mass of plant stems leaving a trail of destruction. In front of them were the otters, ten of them, young ones, ready to fight for their rivers. Next to them were five of the largest, meanest pike you've even seen; they are the biggest fish of the Broads, and their sharp teeth flashed as they opened and closed their mouths. Above them hovered swallows, geese and the peregrine falcon, its sharp talons ready to sink into flesh. The coypu looked at each other. This could be a fight to the finish to decide the fate of the Broads. The coypu bared their large curved yellow teeth and looked mean.

CHAPTER TEN

Confess!

"WHERE IS OUR BOAT?" said the man, looking at the space on the dyke where his little four berth motor cruiser had been berthed.

"It's gone!" said his wife, "Someone's taken it!"

"Let's call the Broads Authority," said the man.

The pair had come back from a long holiday to find their lovely little motor cruiser gone. It was the one Pincher Pete had stolen to carry him and the gang around the southern rivers.

"River Control to all patrols," said the voice from the radio in the Rangers' boat.

"River Control this is River Able," said the Ranger; and one by one all of his colleagues in their boats across the whole of the Broads radioed back to say they were listening.

The officer at River Control in the Broads Authorities HQ told them all to be on the lookout for a small brown Freeman Cruiser, and gave the Broads' registration number, which all boats registered to go on the Broads have and need to display. Soon the boat would be found. The Rangers knew every bit of the Broads and all the rivers and dykes. If something needed finding, they would soon do it. The Broads beat special police unit was alerted too, and they came out on their patrol boat as well to join in the search.

*

"Down here, this little dyke," said the boss as Pincher Pete turned the wheel. They'd just passed a pub on the left – or port – side, and were heading into a shallow little broad called Bargate.

It was getting dark early. The children and *The Little Blue Boat* were a way behind Pincher Pete and his gang because of their speed. The rain had stopped but heavy clouds still made the sky a gun-metal grey.

"Dad will be very worried," said Lucy.

"And very cross," said Alfie.

"I did text him when we couldn't get through because there was no signal back where the treasure was," said Sam.

"Has it gone yet?" asked Lucy.

Alfie went and got the mobile phone. There were ten missed calls.

"Oh no, it was under a cushion we didn't hear it ring!" said Alfie, "What shall we do?"

"Text him again," said Lucy, "at least tell him we're OK but have got delayed, still in search of Teddy."

"And gold and egg thieves and kidnappers!" said Sam.

"Just say Teddy for now," said Lucy as her youngest brother started tapping on the phone keyboard.

"Problem is," said Sam, "the bad guys could have turned off anywhere and we wouldn't know."

"I think we will, somehow I think we will," said Lucy. "Don't ask me why but there's been a kingfisher above us flying all the way. I think, silly as it sounds, but I think it's guiding us."

*

Over at Oulton Broad the Marsh Man stood on the edge of the water looking at the two opposing forces: three hungry, mean-looking coypu on one side and the Marsh Man's friends on the other. Trying a number of rodent languages he spoke to the coypu.

"You can't win. You don't belong here," he said.

"We have no choice!" said the big male coypu, his two female companions either side of him. "We were brought here against our will, we were kidnapped in Italy. We would love to go back to our native South America, but that's impossible so we have to fight to stay and colonise the Broads."

"Wait," said the Marsh Man, "I have a plan. If you promise to put away your teeth and claws and not fight, we can help you get back to South America."

"How?" asked the male coypu.

"Well," said the Marsh Man, "there is a big port called Felixstowe, not fifty miles from here. Each week they have ships, big cargo ships leaving for Brazil. That's a country in South America. If we got you there, you could swim along to one of these boats and stowaway all the way to Brazil."

"Oh that's easy," said the coypu, "we're great swimmers."

"And," said one of his girlfriends next to him, "we can easily climb up anchor ropes and mooring lines and hide in the boat."

"In the bilges, the lowest part of the boat under the floor boards and behind panels," said the other female coypu.

"But," said the male coypu, "could you really get us there?"

"Really," said the Marsh Man. "There are dykes and streams and bits of shoreline between here and the port. Between the otters and our friends the seals in the sea we can guide you. But you need to go and go NOW before the authorities come, or you might not have such a happy ending, they are so scared of your sort, and quite rightly so."

"We never meant to colonise the Broads all those years ago. We coypu never wanted to leave South America, we were brought here because humans wanted to breed us and keep us prisoner so they could kill us for our fur. Some of our ancestors escaped and we have to eat the way we do and that's what caused the trouble," said the big male coypu.

"OK, go, the otters will show you the way. Go now and good luck," said the Marsh Man, and the otters led the three coypu away.

The Marsh Man waved to a passing Ranger whose boat had turned the bend in the river.

"Hello Marsh Man," called out the Ranger, "all OK?"

"Well there was a problem but it's solved now, except I think there's a man in the dyke, a very bad man, who I think you and the police would like to talk to. He has lots to confess. Oh and by the way, if he mentions coypu don't worry, he saw an otter and doesn't know the difference," smiled the Marsh Man.

"Oh that's OK," said the Ranger, "there are no coypu on the Broads now, thank goodness."

"Yes, thank goodness," said the Marsh Man.

The driver was a whimpering wreck, his wet pants pulled up his bum in a wedgie and eels slipping around his wet legs.

"Get me out of here, please, I will confess to everything, just get these horrid things off me!" he squealed. "I'll tell you about the car I stole; the kidnapping of the archaeologist; the bank job when I was twenty; and lots more, just get me out of here, it's horrible!"

The Marsh Man chuckled to himself. "Just one last wedgie?" he laughed and the snakes tugged on the driver's trousers once more.

"Yeooooow!" shouted the driver, "Noooooooo!"

The Marsh Man raised his paddle while the Ranger called the police, and the eels and snakes left the wretched man and slipped away into the dark water.

*

The stolen cruiser was across Bargate, passing the dark, wooden, jagged shapes of sunken wherries on the edge of the water; it was a wherry graveyard.

The Little Blue Boat almost went past the turning, and then Lucy saw something amazing, a row of glow worms lighting the way like airport runway lights. All along the edge of the channel they were evenly spaced, lighting up the route the children needed to take. Glow worms are more like beetles than worms and the females can make their bodies glow a yellow-ish, green-ish light to attract mates. This evening though they were lighting the way for *The Little Blue Boat*.

"It's around here somewhere this bittern's nest," said the boss, looking through the gloom of the approaching dusk. The archaeologist was stuck in the cabin. He noticed a small teddy bear had seemingly found its way into the cabin as well.

Pincher Pete slowed the cruiser down and they crawled slowly along the narrow channel. "It's very shallow around here," he said, "we have to be careful we don't get stuck."

"Yeah," said the smaller of the bad guys, "no one can say I'm a stick in the mud! Ha ha."

"Not funny," said the boss.

"There, it's there," said Pincher Pete, pointing to a clump of reeds with a nest in it and a bittern sitting on top.

"So it is," said the boss, "go for it! We'll nick the eggs, get back to London and we can sell them in the morning."

Pincher Pete stopped the boat.

"There's nowhere to get out?" said Pincher Pete.

"Oh yes there is, look that's a solid bit of ground, just in front of the bittern's nest," said the boss, and he ordered his smaller colleague and Pincher Pete to get out. They did. It was boggy but seemed firm. The boss leaned over and said, "Go and get the eggs then."

As he did, a small Able Sea Bear crawled out of the cabin window and crept along the side of the boat, he stood up to his full height and as the boss was leaning over Teddy pushed his hat which fell into the water.

"Agh!" said the boss, "I've lost my hat!" He leaned over to pick it up and, as he did, Teddy bent down and bit his finger.

"Ouch! I've been bitten, ooohh." The boss fell over the side of the boat and onto his back, on the black, slimy mud at the edge of the reeds below.

Teddy shrunk back quickly, and then undid the catch on the door to release the archaeologist.

Pincher Pete and the smaller of the bad guys got to the nest. The bittern flew off. The nest had five eggs in it. Pincher Pete grabbed them. Each broke with a puff of a very bad smell, a very, very bad smell. They weren't bitterns' eggs; the nest was a decoy. It was a trap. The eggs were old duck eggs, which had failed to hatch and were rotten.

"Oh poo rotten eggs!" shouted Pincher Pete. Then the piece of 'ground' they were standing on started to move. It wasn't solid at all. It was being pulled by something under the water.

"What's happening!" shouted the boss, climbing back to his feet then grabbing hold of his colleague and Pincher Pete, who stunk of rotten eggs.

As the archaeologist climbed out of the cabin, still puzzled as to how the cabin door had suddenly been unlocked, Teddy waved at Pincher Pete.

"That teddy bear – it IS alive!"

"You're mad," said the boss. "And you stink!"

The archaeologist started the motor and drove the motor cruiser a little way away so the gang couldn't get back on board.

Just then *The Little Blue Boat* came down the other dyke that led to Bargate from the River Yare.

"There's Teddy!" shouted Alfie.

"Help!" said the boss, "This ground is breaking up!" And it was, the whole thing had been a trap set by the bitterns; they'd moved their nest and all the eggs and made a decoy nest with old duck eggs. Then they'd got the otters to knit a 'hover' together, a collection of reeds which looked solid but which really wasn't. Now the otters were under the water breaking it up, soon the gang of three were waist high in thick, dark mud. Stuck fast, there was no escape.

"HELP! We'll drown!" shouted the boss.

"Rescue us and we'll tell you everything!" shouted Pincher Pete.

The archaeologist told the children to keep away from the men as they were dangerous criminals, and then he threw a rope to the men in the water.

"Hold on to the rope," said the archaeologist, "but I'll only pull you out if you confess your crimes."

Lucy dialled the police on the mobile.

"Hello officer," she said, "please listen to this: I have Pincher Pete and some friends who have things to tell you. Please get someone here as soon as you can, we're at Bargate off the River Yare, there's a stolen cruiser and a kidnap victim."

Pincher Pete blabbed like a baby, telling the police officer on the end of the phone everything the gang had done and more.

Just then the Rangers and the Broads beat officers

arrived and took over. They arrested the men who were pulled from the thick mud smelling badly and cold and wet. As they did, Teddy climbed down and grabbed the boss's hat without anyone seeing. He bit the rim of the hat hard and threw it on the floor of the Rangers' boat. One of the Rangers picked it up and a piece of paper fell out of the rim. "This is interesting," he said. "It's a list of the names and addresses of all the birds' eggs thieves in Britain!"

"Thank you children you've done a great job," said the other Ranger as the police handcuffed the gang. "There is someone who will be glad to see you, and don't worry he's not cross."

The children's dad came out of the Rangers' boat and waved.

On the shore watching through the reeds was the Marsh Man, smiling. He laughed, raised his paddle and nodded towards the sky. Then the peregrine falcon swooped down and dropped something into the cockpit of the stolen cruiser where the archaeologist was standing. It was the gold torque.

Alfie gasped, "The Viking gold!"

"No," said Lucy, "the Marsh Man's gold."

"This is going to Norwich museum so everyone can enjoy it," said the archaeologist.

"I want to be an archy-olo-arhi-ol… someone who digs up the past when I grow up," said Alfie.

"I want to be a Ranger or a policeman," said Sam.

"And I want to be a sailor," said Lucy. *I also want to know who the Marsh Man really is*, she thought to herself.

"I want porridge for breakfast," said Pincher Pete, "it's prison for us, but please don't make me share a cell with these two."

"No fear," said the boss, "you stink!"

The archaeologist picked Teddy up from the floor of the stolen cruiser and passed him to *The Little Blue Boat*. Alfie grabbed him and cuddled him hard.

"Oh Teddy I'm never going to let you out of my sight again!"

"Nor me," said Sam. "However much you smell of the river!"

Lucy smiled and patted Teddy's head. Teddy so wanted to cuddle them back and tell them of his adventures but knew he couldn't.

*

A few weeks later *The Little Blue Boat* was back in the boat yard near Barton Broad. The children were in Norwich at the official hand-over of the golden torque to the museum, and were being photographed with the archaeologist by the *Eastern Daily Press* and the local ITV and BBC news programmes. They were treated like stars with Radio Norfolk and the rest of the local media all queuing up to talk to them about their adventure.

Able Sea Bear Teddy sat back in the cockpit looking at the swallows flying high above. He smiled. A large sea bird landed on the coach roof of *The Little Blue Boat*.

"Got any marmite sandwiches?" said the gull.

"We like sandwiches, especially marmite sandwiches," said his gull friend.

Teddy smiled and fell asleep in the sun, remembering how his whole Broads adventure had started, and all the friends he'd made along the way.

Animal and Bird Biographies

Bat

• The bat in our story is a common pipistrelle. It's one of Britain's most common bats. One of the best times to see them is soon after the sun sets.

• These bats like to live in a number of places including woodland and farmland as well as in some buildings.

• Old churches and barn roofs are also quite popular choices for bats' homes.

• Bats use an echo location system to find their way around. They send out a high pitched noise which bounces back when it hits something, so the bat can work out where things are.

• Bats' favourite food includes small flies like mosquitoes and midges.

• Bats are protected by law making it illegal to capture, hurt or kill them.

Kingfisher

- These beautiful birds have green-ish, blue and orange colourings.
- Kingfishers like to live by still or slow flowing water, rivers, broads and lakes.
- These birds are quite shy and can often be seen darting from bush to bush near water. They often sit on low branches or hover above the water before catching their food.
- Kingfishers' favourite foods are fish, such as minnows and sticklebacks; as well as some insects and freshwater shrimps.
- These birds are protected by law, and it's illegal to hurt or kill them, or to disturb or take away their nests.

Water vole

• These aquatic rodents are similar to rats, but they have rounder noses, deep brown fur, chubby faces and, unlike rats they have hairy tails, paws and ears!

• Water voles like to live on the banks of rivers, streams and dykes; as well as reed beds by slow moving water, broads and lakes.

• Their favourite foods include plants and grass near the water, as well as some fruits, bulbs, twigs and roots.

• The number of water voles has fallen rapidly in recent decades and it is now against the law to hurt or kill them, or to destroy their homes.

Swallows

• These small birds have dark, glossy-blue backs, with red throats, pale tummies and long tails.
• Swallows live in many parts of this country during the summer, but they prefer to fly south to migrate to warmer areas for the cold winter months.
• These birds' favourite foods are insects, like mosquitoes and midges, which they usually catch while flying.
• Swallows love to build nests under eaves of buildings and in dark ledges, nooks and crannies.
• Swallows are protected by law. It is illegal to hurt or kill them or to destroy or damage their nests or eggs.

Chinese Water Deer

• Originally these animals came from China and Korea and were first introduced into Britain in the late 1800s. They were kept in zoos and wildlife collections but some escaped! They are mostly found in eastern England and especially in Norfolk where they like the habitat around the Broads.

• These small deer like to eat the plants and herbs that grow in wetlands and near rivers and broads.

• Chinese Water Deer are very good at swimming, and are thought to be able to swim for several miles if they need to.

• The males don't have antlers like other, larger species of deer, but instead they have long canine teeth which are like little tusks.

Grass Snake

• These snakes are the UK's largest reptile, and they lay eggs.

• Grass snakes are usually a green-ish colour, and have a yellow ring behind their head. They also have black patches on their necks. They can grow up to two metres long.

• These snakes like living on the edges of woodland and near water. They are very strong swimmers and can be seen crossing broads, rivers and lakes. Their favourite foods include toads, frogs and some fish.

• Grass snakes are not poisonous and are harmless to humans, unlike some other snakes.

• Grass snakes are protected by law. It's is illegal to hurt, capture or kill them.

Peregrine Falcon

• These are said to be possibly the fastest birds in the world. They are believed to be able to fly at two hundred miles an hour.
• Peregrines like to live by open countryside, but they also like tall buildings in towns and cities.
• Peregrine falcons eat other birds like pigeons and small ducks. They have very sharp talons or claws.
• Peregrine Falcons can be found in all parts of the world except for Polar Regions.
• These birds are also protected by law and it is illegal to capture, hurt or kill them.

You will find me with the sun's rise and the night's fall.

I am there with the cold winter wind and the warm summer breeze.

I will be near the water and the wildlife, by the wind and the waves

I walk the pretty little paths, and sit on watery banks.

I am here in the sunshine and in the storms.

I know the secrets and the mysteries of the rivers and the Broads.

For I, am the Marsh Man.

Also available in this series by the same author is
The Little Blue Boat and the Secret of the Broads!

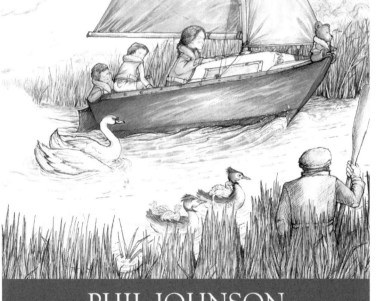

The
Little Blue
Boat

AND THE SECRET OF THE BROADS!

PHIL JOHNSON
ILLUSTRATED BY PAUL JACKSON